~ Siren ~

In Greek mythologies, Sirens were beautiful and dangerous creatures who lured sailors with their enchanting music and voices to shipwreck on the rocky coast of their island. The Sirens were highly feared, yet coveted. It was believed that no-one was immune to her charms.

Leonardo da Vinci once wrote of the Siren, "The siren sings so sweetly that she lulls the mariners to sleep; then she climbs upon the ships and kills the sleeping mariners."

Franz Kafka wrote in The Silence of the Sirens, "Now the Sirens have a still more fatal weapon than their song, namely their silence. And though admittedly such a thing never happened, it was still conceivable that someone might possibly have escaped from their singing; but from their silence certainly never."

SIREN

JO-ANNE JOSEPH

DEDICATION

To *you,*

To every part of, and the whole of *you,*

For every struggle *you've* been through,

For every battle *you* have survived,

Look how far *you've* come,

See how brave *you've* been,

I see *you,*

I know.

Prologue

The last few months had been a haze. I'd constantly been wandering around in a dreamlike state. I feared going to sleep at night, yet fought the urge to wake up the next day, because nothing, absolutely nothing, made any sense anymore. The life that was once my *reality* became a blur. Every version of it slipped and faded into each other until I couldn't tell what was real and what wasn't. I tried to convince myself that every time I woke up, I would be closer to rationalizing my dreams from truth or at least finding some order in all this chaos.

I wanted to be able to set apart the lies from everything else, I needed to, but doing that seemed impossible for me. I yearned to get to a point in my thoughts where everything that had ever happened to me, everything that I'd been through started to make an ounce of sense. I always felt that if I couldn't fuse the planes, which only I seemed to have existed on, then I should at least be able to see noticeable differences between them.

In time though, I realized that there wasn't just here and there or this place and that. Where the decidedly sane and rational existed or where those on the other end of the continuum were. No, there were many realms of existence, something the world found difficult to acknowledge and accept. Perhaps it was the fear of the unknown, it could be disbelief, or maybe, just maybe, it was because we were all there, in that place in between waiting to slip back into illusion or move forward to face a truth which was sometimes hard to stomach.

I am Sage, and this is my story.

I stared at myself in the mirror. I looked like I'd been dragged through the depths of hell. My jet-colored eyes were hollow. The black rings around them gave me a haunted look which I found appropriate given that I was only a ghost of the woman I once was. My cheekbones were accentuated; my skin was sallow, lifelessly pale. I feared that if I touched it, it would disintegrate at my fingertips. My once long raven tresses had been cut short and rested on my shoulders because *they* feared I'd use its length to hurt myself. But no pain could be worse than *this*. I was a prisoner in my own hell, and I had no way out.

My faded blue dress hung limply on my lanky frame, and my hip bones jutted out hideously. I tugged on the cotton fabric which felt rough and over-starched. These were the only clothes I owned and the only ones I was allowed to wear. My arms and legs were the worst. A thin layer of flesh covered it, but barely. I could see the blue-green in my veins. I wanted to claw at the image before me, claw at it until nothing remained, until I wiped every trace of this monstrosity from my sight. I'd never been a vain person, but this creature that's staring back at me wasn't me. I sighed and looked away from the image, appalled.

My routine never changed. I woke up at five a.m. every morning. There was no such thing as sleeping in here, not even on the weekend. This was followed by a strip search and a thorough exploration of the four-walled space they referred to as my accommodation. There wasn't much to find in here. It's a generic four white-walled room with small barred windows which were sealed shut. The bars were so close together; I couldn't even stick my fingers through them, they shouldn't have bothered trying to let the light in.

Light cannot exist in a place where darkness reigned supreme.

There's a single bed with cheap white cotton linen as overly starched as the dresses I wore. A small side table with no drawers sat beside the bed. The writing desk which also had no drawers was in the far corner, and I was sure it was simply there for display as we have no access to stationery. A rigid wooden chair was set before the table.

There was no reading lamp, and the lights were controlled centrally. When the lights go out, it's time for bed, and there was no room for negotiation. I have a few of my favorite books lined on a shelf, but I haven't found the will to read them. It wasn't a lack of time; there was too much of it here, but rather, a lack of motivation. I'd stare at one page for hours. The words faded into each other making it difficult to comprehend. The stories merged into one another so much it left me confused.

There was a wardrobe without a door on one side of the room. In it hung an assortment of dresses much like the one I have on, in various matching shades. I was indifferent to them all. In my old room, from where I come, there were rows of clothing in a walk-in closet in various colors and styles, but there was no place for that here. Even my cotton panties are on display for the world to see.

I looked up at the camera, the one that looked like an alarm system eyelet and wondered what they're doing on the other side. I knew better than to assume it's not recording my every move. I wanted to give them a show, let them know I knew, but instead I stared until my eyes hurt. I was in a place like this a while ago, and the lay of the land doesn't change.

They gave me *private* time, but I didn't understand the logic in pretending that they weren't watching because they were. All the time.

I attended the gym for an hour with my designated group of peers. That too changed from time to time. We were not allowed to interact for extended periods of time with any of the other *inmates*, and I used that term loosely. They shouldn't worry about things like that though, that isn't even a risk. Nobody was ever in a socializing mood, much less in a mood to discuss the overthrow of a place like this.

I didn't know the stories behind those vacant eyes, but I knew mine, and unlike the rest of them, I was here by choice. By my own free will that gets chipped away a little every single day. I am here physically, but emotionally I was not. We were all shackled to the rhythm, and we didn't want any trouble because it caused more pain and we could all do without it. The pain I felt ran deeper than the physical, no amount of shock therapy could compare to the scars on my mind.

I, like everyone else here, showered for five minutes exactly. That was the only time I was allowed to be completely alone. This was supposedly the only area in this hellhole where there were no cameras. That and the toilets, which I was also permitted five to ten minutes depending on the business I needed to conduct in there. Someone was stationed at the door at all times to make sure we stuck to the agreed duration of time allocated to us. If we're a minute over, they barged in, and we risked exposure.

There was no such thing as privacy in a place like this. We gave up our right to that the minute we arrived. We signed our lives over to them, and they were sworn to protect it.

You could lose track of time behind these walls, maybe I've been here a year, maybe five, who knew. All I was certain of was that I was fading away in here.

There was a communal silent lunch consisting of bland chicken or steak served with vegetables or salad. There was no sound of clanking of silverware on porcelain plates. We were handed plastic spoons and knives which we handed back in once we're done eating. We took our second round of medication after lunch, and were sent back to our rooms where we waited for our *saviors*. They swooped in with their white coats, notepads and sharpened pencils proceeding to waste two hours of time trying to understand us, to help us and to ultimately redeem us. But there was no redemption here, not for me or any of the lost souls around me. They suggested all kinds of treatments and medications which would supposedly allow us to *help* ourselves. They assured us that this was not a prison, but that didn't explain the bolts on our doors or the chains on our souls.

This was my life.

This was my lot.

And this was how I would spend the rest of my days.

I have a vague recollection of existence before this. Life outside of this *prison*, but it's much too scary to think about sometimes.

The fact that I find myself in this hellhole cannot be real. I spent my days mentally journaling my every thought in the hope that someday I could decipher what was real and what wasn't and maybe I'd be able to live a life that meant something again.

It is not about fighting the darkness,
But rather, embracing the light.

Once upon a time…

The little girl cried silently into her pillow. The monsters were everywhere. She could hear them laughing in the other room, she heard them all around her. They seemed to be edging closer and closer. She peeked up from under the covers and saw a sliver of light from under the door. The light scared her even more than the darkness. It meant that they would come. She hid her head under the covers again. Pulling them up tight around her, she prayed that maybe if she were quiet enough, they wouldn't be able to hear her. They would forget that she existed and leave her alone. She wished she had superpowers, like in the comics, and then she would shrink herself small and crawl under that door and go away from here. She could imagine doing that. This little house was always full of people. So many people everywhere and all the time. And then there were the monsters and the screams. They were laughing and jeering and she could hear the woman crying, crying, and crying…why was she always crying? The woman had the same hair as she did, but her eyes were different, cold, with a glimpse of cruelty behind them. She was a ghost woman. A scary ghost woman. If she tried hard enough, maybe, she could wish the ghost and monsters away.

My parents died. I didn't.

I was there when it happened, and yet, I didn't remember a damn thing. It felt like that part of my memory was erased permanently. I racked my brain, and no matter how hard I tried, I couldn't remember. So, after a while, I stopped trying to remember because it hurt too much. The pain became unbearable. The anger became harder to control.

My earliest recollection started with me waking up in a hospital, afraid and distraught wondering where I was and where my Mom and Dad were. How did I get from sitting on the sand with my mother, her long brown hair whipping around her face as she smiled down at me, to this sterile and cold room?

I looked over to where my sister Siren was asleep, on the bed across from me. Her long ebony hair was splayed across the pillow and covered most of her face which was a replica of my own. For a second, I wondered whether she was still alive. But she stirred and I breathed a sigh of relief.

I still remembered the sound of the rain pelting down on the hospital windows and the sound of the machines I was hooked up to. There was a pain in my hand where the needle of the drip pierced through my flesh. I tried to move my other arm, but it hurt too much. The strong smell of the antiseptic was thick in the air. It burnt my nose causing me to wrinkle it up in discomfort.

The doctors and nurses came in to check on me every half an hour.

"Are you alright, Sage?" they'd ask. I never responded because no words came.

Everyone regarded me with pity. I knew that was the one look I wouldn't miss when I finally got to leave this place.

My grandparents, who were no more than strangers to me, arrived. My grandmother held my hand as they both flanked either side of my hospital bed, and told me that my parents had died.

"They're in heaven now," my grandmother whispered. She was a frail lady with gray hair and more wrinkles than I could count. I'd only seen her a few times before that day in the hospital. She tried to convince me that the reason I'd survived was that there was so much more for me to do in life. She patted my hand which was hooked up to the drip, and I felt nothing. Instead, I concentrated on her eyes which were welling with tears. She never looked me directly in the eye once. It was as if she could see right through me; like I was not even there and yet I was right in front of her. And so I didn't speak to her either. She made me feel invisible.

There had to be some mistake. I couldn't do all this without my parents. I needed them. They were all my sister and I had in this world. Our family has always been all we ever needed. My cries echoed off the walls, and I was sure that they could be heard all through the hospital ward. Before long, doctors and nurses rushed into the room. The tears flowed down my cheeks, and I was sure that there was enough to cause a flood. I was distraught, and I wanted my family back. Unfortunately, my *once upon a time* ended long before it began and as the needles dug into my soft skin, I let myself drift off because oblivion was better than facing a life without them.

Take me back to where it all began,
To childhood,
To that place of no complications,
Where there was no sadness,
No injustice,
Take me back to the sun,
Let it shine brighter in my sky again.

ONE
SAGE

NEW BEGINNINGS...

Siren and I moved in with our grandparents a week after I woke up in hospital. They were our only surviving family. A ten-year-old shouldn't hate life, but I did. My grandparents were in their late sixties, and their views of life and everything, in general, were outdated. Our parents were both only children and our paternal grandparents had died long before we were born. In our house, entertainment was limited to watching something on the obsolete television or me reading in my room alone. It was the nineties, and we didn't even have a VCR.

My grandfather was a tall and gangly man with hip and back problems, so he never did much more than lounge around reading the newspaper. He would cough and splutter every time he moved an inch which meant he didn't move at all. He never took me anywhere, not to the mall or any of the fairs that came to our small town now and then. I wondered how it was possible for my mother to grow up here, in this town where nothing ever seemed to happen. I felt suffocated and alone. My extensive knowledge of this town came from walking from my front porch to school and then back again. Thankfully we never could afford transportation to school; otherwise, I would have died of boredom because I would have seen even less of the real world. That didn't seem like such a bad idea though, not for me. Death seemed like a far better destination than this meaningless existence which was handed to me. I often wondered what would happen if I did die. Would anyone miss me? Or would my grandparents simply move on with their dull lives with one less complication to worry about?

My grandmother cried every time she looked at me in that first year I lived with them, and it infuriated me. I got that she missed my Mom, I got that, but I'd lost so much more than she had. She wouldn't even begin to understand what I was going through.

"Every time I look at you, I'm reminded of my daughter. She loved you so much Sage. I miss her every day," she sobbed. I felt like there was so much more to her behavior than she let on, but I didn't bother asking. I didn't care.

I sensed that Siren and I were a grave inconvenience to my grandparents and that made me miss my parents so much more. I felt alone and abandoned.

I didn't understand why people as kind and wonderful as they had to die. They were the kind of parents that the children in our old neighborhood adored. We tended to move around a lot but no matter where we went, we laid down roots, and we always fit in. And even if we didn't fit in, we still had each other, and that was what counted. I always thought that people were supposed to grow to a ripe old age, but fate had other plans for us.

But was it fate?

Were things meant to be this way?

Or was this all part of a carefully orchestrated plan to destroy a young girl's life.

Whenever I thought about them, I would sink into sadness. I'd lost a part of my soul the day I lost them. A part of me I would never get back. I missed their smiles and easy laughter. The kisses goodnight and all the special things they did to make us feel like we were the center of their universe. Siren discouraged me from thinking or talking about them too much. She said that if I carried around that grief, it would swallow me whole. She didn't realize that it already had. I'd sunken into the pit of despair, and I was no longer the child I used to be. I grew up too fast, unwillingly.

Siren urged me to push all thoughts of them to the deepest darkest part of my memory so I could be happy again. It's what she'd done, and she was better off for it. I didn't comprehend how I would ever be happy again. I also couldn't understand how she could be so blasé about it either. They were her parents too. They loved us with everything they had. They didn't just tell us, they showed us and we knew. I knew she knew, I could tell.

Moving here meant leaving behind my home and friends. Everything I knew and loved was gone. I didn't have any friends in this town. People don't treat you the same way they treat others when you're an outsider and not having a *normal* family didn't help. I don't know why it was like that, but it was the way things were around here.

We were treated like we were the plagues of Egypt, ready to be unleashed upon them, destroying their seemingly perfect lives. Perhaps they feared the great sadness which haunted my eyes would find them. Or they simply couldn't deal with us because they knew of our loss. Once you were burdened with losing a loved one, you carried it around like the weight of the world.

I was grateful to have my sister despite the fact that she was a bully at times. I never understood that either. She wanted me to do everything the way she told me to. More often than not I was told that if I didn't, we'd get thrown into a home for orphan children. Deep down I knew that it wouldn't matter how we behaved anyway because if our already ancient grandparents died, we'd be out on the streets before the funeral. I told her just that, and it made her angry, earning me a slap which left a red mark on my cheek and split my lip.

Later that night at dinner, grandma asked me what had happened to my face and I told her the truth earning a glare from Siren from across the room. It didn't faze her though, and she continued eating her dinner as if she hadn't heard a word I uttered.

"Now, now Sage, you know that lies are not allowed in this house," my grandmother warned narrowing her eyes at me while she waved around a spoon full of mash potato.

"But she did," I insisted. "Own up Siren." I stared at her imploring her to tell the truth.

She just sat there with a grin on her face. I wanted to go over there and wipe it right off.

"Siren didn't do that, you know that Sage," my grandfather growled.

"This is so frustrating," I murmured.

"Go to your room Sage, I will not have insolence at the dinner table," my grandmother demanded.

That was the first of many times I got into trouble for Siren over the years. I started to dislike her as we grew older, and it only caused her to try to control me more, especially in our teenage years. Before I knew it, she was making all my decisions, good and bad, and I was sinking deeper into myself with no hope of recovery. I didn't have a chance against her. She was more popular, more beautiful, smarter, tougher and everything that I wasn't. People loved her. I watched her walk around the school as if she owned it. In our senior year, she was the one who became valedictorian. She reminded me that she was better than me, every single day. If I fought back, she would hurt me and every time I told on her; I got reprimanded.

"You can't blame everything on Siren, Sage," my grandmother admonished. "When are you going to take responsibility for your own actions?" I would walk away and listen to their hushed whispers about my behavior. I heard Siren milk every drop of sympathy from my grandparents.

Very soon I lost my own voice; I just did as I was told and that kept me sane.

"You're acting weird, Sage. People are going to think you're losing your mind." Siren taunted me. She sat on the hammock in the backyard, reading one of those teen magazines the cool kids were into. I knew there was some truth to her words. The other kids called me a zombie, weird.

I hated my life and every day I wished for a different one, like the ones in the movies, where everyone could live their dreams and do whatever they wanted to. Children had both their parents and every day was one big fairytale. I wanted to get away from here, away from all this. Find someplace where I belonged.

"People like you shouldn't dream because none of them will ever come true." She sneered bouncing her glitter ball off the ceiling one night.

I guess she was right, if dreams did come true, I would be Siren, and maybe there wouldn't be me at all.

Stay quiet little one,
don't come out to play,
and if you play,
play silently,
they are listening,
they are watching
they are lurking
I can't help you
Unless you're still…

TWO
SAGE

PRESENT DAY

The house was deathly quiet, and the little girl bent to get her dolls from under the bed. They were her special dolls, and she was sure not to take them out of their hiding place when he was around. She shouldn't share these treasures with anyone. They reminded her of a time long ago when she was laughing on the sand. It was hard to remember if that was a memory or a dream. It must be a dream. Ghost woman had told her that much.

"Brat, get in here and do the fucking dishes," he shouted from somewhere in the house.

The little girl was startled which caused her to drop her dolls to the ground. She must keep them hidden away, that was the only way to protect them. The chills ran up her back and neck when she heard his footsteps and voice edging closer. He seemed angrier today. She could hear it by the heaviness of every step on the wooden floors in the hallway, as he got closer. She hated the woman, but she hated this monster even more. He was pure evil, she knew it. She saw it in his eyes, and in the way, he looked at her. One day she would grow up and put a stake in his evil heart, and she would laugh as those actors did in the movies the woman watched. She laughed now, laughed so hard that she didn't hear the monster behind her until it

The frequency of the dreams was getting more regular. I started having them since I was a teenager. They were not anything to be concerned about then, but now, years later, they were a nightly occurrence, and there was nothing I could do to stop them. The world of dreams was not something that we can control. I didn't understand what these dreams meant. I didn't recognize the people I was dreaming about. I'd never seen them in my life.

All I knew was that in those dreams, I was that little girl and I was terrified.

I felt her fear.

I felt it deep inside me.

But, that didn't make any sense because I had never encountered anything even remotely close to what I dreamed of. There were things I'd forgotten about, like the accident I was in with my parents, but everything before and after the accident seemed clearer now. I wondered if I was having some kind of out of body experience. That would explain why the dreams felt so real.

I sat at the kitchen table sipping my first cup of tea for the day, a strawberry tea blend, one sugar, no milk and studied the woman sitting across from me. Her beautiful black hair was styled to perfection and fell over both her shoulders like a shroud. She always wore a minimal amount of makeup, but she was without a doubt the most beautiful woman I have ever laid my eyes on. She was a classic beauty. Her black eyes were large, the kind that would entice one to follow her to the ends of the earth. The eyelashes kissed her cheeks every time she blinked. Her legs were long and her body lean. She went to the gym at least five days a week and always dressed immaculately. Her outfits were designed by the most renowned designers in the country. She would never be seen wearing the same outfit twice or without her killer heels. Her heels were so high; I could probably use them to put up another bookshelf in my room. She flicked a bit of her long hair over her shoulder, and it glistened in the morning light. Her eyes did not move from the newspaper she was reading. Her back was straight, vanity oozed off her. She picked up her third cup of espresso and downed it without flinching. She slid the small cup and saucer on the table, away from herself without making a sound.

"Stay up to date with the world Sage and you'll never get left behind." My sister often criticized me.

I wished I could talk to her about the dreams. They were important to me. My hands quivered slightly whenever I brought my cup up to my lips, causing a clattering sound and she regarded me with distaste. The silence in the room was palpable, but despite the fact that I was a grown ass woman, I do not speak unless I am spoken to, just another one of her rules, which must be adhered to at all times. I hated when I displeased her, it always made me feel worse about myself. I looked down at my drab gray sweater which had seen better days, covered by my signature black hoodie and my dark skinny jeans and Chuck Taylors. I screamed plain, Plain Sage. Sometimes I wish I could be more like Siren and at other times I'm glad I'm not.

"You should dress better Sage, maybe add some color. You fade into the background." She bit out suddenly looking at me with revulsion. I wondered if she could read my mind sometimes. I looked at her, but don't bother responding. How does one respond to that kind of criticism anyway? She's right about me. I did fade into the background. Hardly anyone noticed me.

She cocked an eyebrow assessing me, no doubt trying to read my thoughts. "We have to go, clear up will you," she sighed, getting up and meticulously folding her newspaper, setting it aside. "Make sure you behave today." She ordered calmly. When she spoke to me like that she made me feel like an invalid. I hated it, but there was nothing that I can do about it. I was at her mercy, and I have given her that kind of power over me.

So instead of telling her to go to hell, I responded the only way I knew how. "I will Siren." I picked up our cups, rinsed them off and left them on the basin to dry. This kitchen was sterile and cold, white and stainless steel. It reminded me of a hospital instead of a kitchen. But the rule was *cleanliness is perfections son* and Siren has had a long-standing love affair with it. I chuckled to myself.

I watched her as she made her way to her bedroom. Her heels clicked on the porcelain tiles of the hallway. She occupied the master bedroom in *our* two bedroom apartment; one wall was completely glass and had the most magnificent view of the city. We lived in Cape

Town, the city that never sleeps, always abuzz with life pulsing through its veins. This place was nothing like where we grew up, but we moved here after college, and it's where Siren decided to settle down in. The rest of her room had floor to ceiling mirrors as if narcissism were a source of life. She had a king size bed with white and red linen. It dripped with sex appeal, but she never brought anyone into this apartment. Visitors were not allowed into Siren's sanctuary. I did not believe for a second that she wasn't fucking every man who gave her a second glance, which was every second one and yet, she had never dated anyone. I'm not surprised though. I doubted anyone could handle the psycho Siren. She was self-absorbed and selfish with just the right amount of fucking insane.

Everything in this apartment screamed Siren. Warmth evaded this living space. There was no trace of me here. It was as if I didn't exist in her perfect world. I was just a bystander in the life and times of Siren Fenton. Still, I was happy with my dull existence, my boring bedroom which thankfully had a bathroom of my own which meant that I didn't have to share with Siren. I didn't want to hear about my tardiness any more than I do right now. I have a queen size bed with gray and purple covers, a writing desk and a floor to ceiling bookshelf. There isn't much else a girl needs anyway. Well, this girl at least.

Sage and Siren, sisters, twins, but looking at us you wouldn't think so. Yes, there are the obvious similarities in our outer appearance, but we are nothing alike. We don't talk in the same way. We don't behave in the same way. We have no similar interests. We are opposites. No wonder my parents named me Sage, the gentle garden herb, and her Siren, the beautiful creature whose singing lured unwary sailors onto rocks to their deaths.

Siren has been with me my whole life. It wasn't just because she was the only close family I had left but because she could not, or rather would not, release me from her clutches. She was in charge, and if I was honest with myself, I'd admit that I was afraid. I'm terrified of what she's done and what she will do, of what her abuse will eventually do to my mind. I felt myself already cracking, and I'm scared that one more hit, will cause me to fall apart. Sometimes, I wondered whether Siren would have acted differently towards me if our parents were still alive. Would she love me? Would we be friends? Did she treat me the way she did because she felt responsible for her mentally unstable sister? This was what everyone thinks about me, and my grandparents didn't make the situation any easier by constantly siding with her when we were growing up. My state of mind made it possible for her to belittle me, making me feel like less of a human. This was a game to her. Abuse Sage and then make her feel like it is all her fault. I was on that hamster wheel going round and round.

But that was something I didn't want to dwell on. I couldn't change it even if I wanted to. I'm indebted to her. I always would be. She reminded me of that every day. I would always be unworthy. What's done is done. It was water under the bridge. It is what it is.

I pulled on my heavy coat and glanced at the large wall clock. We leave at exactly eight every morning and drive to our common workplace. Siren is a control freak, and it isn't enough that we live together, we have to work together too so that she could keep an eye on me. I waited in anticipation at the door. She brushed past me, and I followed her obediently. I couldn't help but twist my sleeves anxiously on the drive to the office, causing her to glare at me. Every day out in the world is a battle of epic proportions. I feel my skin starting to itch, my ears starting to burn, and I knew that if I didn't breathe deeply enough I'd have a panic attack and I would not give her that satisfaction. I've become tired of playing the fool.

Siren is a successful PR executive. She was supposedly the best the business had to offer. I was of course a meager filing clerk in the editorial department. I'm not complaining, it paid, not that I had any need for money, but at least I didn't have to see her for a few hours a day being based on a different floor. It's the only time in the day when I felt like I could breathe. I could be me without fear of judgment. We entered the parking lot in her blue Mercedes Benz E Class, no less for the Princess. I jumped out while one of the porters opened her door for her. He's a tall man, burly; his dark skin glistened when she looked at him. She made them all nervous. I could sense his fear and fascination. He held the door open for her, slightly cowering.

"Good morning, Ms. Fenton," he greeted in a deep rumble. She nodded at him haughtily in response, and I pulled my jacket hood further over my head to cover my face and shrank away. I was not allowed to talk to anyone at the office unless it has to do with work because according to my sister, anyone dumb enough to speak to me wants to probe me for information about Siren. She's paranoid about these things; I have come to realize that, so I won't say or do anything that will ever make her angry. If I did, I knew that I would regret it.

Who would want to socialize with me anyway? I wasn't the kind of woman that got any attention unless it was negative and condescending. Sometimes it felt like I'd never left high school. I was always that girl at the back of the line and the last one anyone was ever going to pick.

We climbed into the elevator, and she started to run through the do's and don'ts of my day.

DO work to the best of your ability.

DO NOT cause me shame and embarrassment by failing.

Failure is not an option.

DO act overly pleasant to colleagues.

DO NOT make friends.

Friends will hurt and use you.

Friends will destroy you.

I listened to her rambling and nod. My palms had already started sweating. I heard this mantra every day. But for some reason, today, she seemed even more agitated than usual. I tried to ignore it as I exited the elevator on my floor. I can't begin to understand what goes on in that mind of hers.

"Get out of your head, Sage," she hissed. I don't sass her the way I want to. I don't even say goodbye. I simply back away in case someone sees me with her, but I watch as the elevator closed her in, as I always do, wishing that she would disappear from my life for good. She doesn't associate with people in my department which I was relieved about, we, fortunately, do not meet Siren's A-list, but who the fuck cares, that list was so short anyway. But, her escapades with my boss Steve a few years ago didn't go unnoticed, especially not by me. I walked straight ahead and plopped myself down on my chair at the window, finally able to breathe. I swiveled in my chair and stared out of the window, glancing at the side of the building next to this one and imagining it's the ocean, calming my nerves, the smell filling my senses. One day I would leave here. I would get on a bus and get the hell away from this miserable excuse called my life. I deserved that at least. I don't care if I was a beggar on the streets. Anything was better than this, a life controlled and manipulated by another person. I had no control of anything.

"Sage!" my boss Steve called. "This isn't the time to be daydreaming," he grunted. "Get your act together, Fenton."

I didn't even realize I'd been out of it for that long. Steve was in his mid-forties, he's a tall, overpowering man who doesn't look a day older than thirty. His hair was still dark and full, and he uses the company gym at least four days a week. His black eyes are kind, and he isn't as scary as he thinks he is. I saw the concern etched on his face when I arrived here bruised after one of Sirens outbursts. I'd come to consider him as a friend, not just a boss. He was strict, wanting to ensure that our team got the job done. Our deadlines were tight, and it made him uptight and edgy. But still, he was a good man and I wondered how he ever got mixed up with Siren, but there have not been many who could resist her charms if you could call it that.

"Sorry, Steve," I responded keeping my head down, not wanting to meet his gaze.

I'm always afraid that he'll get tired of me and fire me. I couldn't get fired no matter how much I disliked Steve and his abruptness sometimes. Siren wouldn't approve of that. The thing she hated the most was disappointment, and that is all I have ever been to her. But besides the fact that she'd be upset, this was the only place I seemed to fit in, amongst the dust and pages was where my heart resided.

THREE

JAKE

I hated this dull, dreary, rainy weather. It always reminded me of a place I had long since left behind and I tried every single day to forget. Home. Well, I couldn't call it that anymore. It hadn't felt like home for several years before I left. I reminded myself that today was not the day to dwell on the past. This was my moment. I was stepping into a new phase of my life. Tomorrow I would be starting a new job at a huge publication company, a giant amongst giants. I'd studied long and hard, and now I would be an Assistant Editor. This was the life, I think. The kind of thing my parents would be so proud of, I add sarcastically. The achievement they could gloat about at their fancy dinner parties, in between the latest heart my brother successfully transplanted, and the high power case my sister just won. I could see it now, Jake the *Assistant* Editor. The truth was that this was huge to me, something I have only ever dreamt of.

I was not bitter about my family's views on it, not anymore. But the way they belittled anything that had my name attached to it still sent a sliver of frustration racing through me from time to time. I do not have that typical middle child inferiority complex some people have, making them crawl into themselves accepting defeat, even though technically I was the middle child. I have always wanted to do my own thing, and I didn't care if it didn't fit into the Cole family mold.

There was my father, the highest paid plastic surgeon in the country who worked with celebrities on a daily basis gifting them with the perfect nose or set of tits so big there wasn't a bra on earth that would hold them. Michael Cole, the household name, the magician.

My mother, Catherine Cole, was the most renowned chiropractor, her fame was considerably low key, but she was still highly successful. She'd been on numerous talk shows and written a dozen books on neck care, back care and every other kind of care.

My sister, Melissa, was a hotshot criminal attorney who'd been seen on TV more than a few times. But the real family celebrity and the star of the show was my older brother Derrick Cole, the heart surgeon, with a heart as everyone described him. It didn't help that they were all perfect.

There was a gene pool of power and talent, and then, there was *me*, Jacob Cole, the dreamer, the writer, the poet, and the English Literature major. It wasn't because there was too much expectation placed on me that I never followed in their footsteps, but rather that there was too little. I was treated like the middle child, but I never felt like it, instead I felt free, so much so that I was pretty happy about it growing up. I was content doing my own thing, finding my way in this world.

That was until the insults started and the insinuation

that I was the runt of the litter.

"It's a pity he hasn't lived up to his brilliant family name." Family and friends would whisper at parties, "It is such a pity that he isn't as bright as the other two children. Odd isn't it?"

My Father would drink to that or laugh it off. I often wondered how a parent could listen to such insults about his child and say nothing. It was then that I realized that he felt the same way they did. I would always be a disappointment to *the* Michael Cole. So I stopped trying to convince everyone otherwise.

And this was why I found myself here in Cape Town, a few hours away from my hometown, ready to do what it took to make it to the top on my own, away from anyone who knew me. Now I could earn my own way and do what I did best, edit and write. There were so many stories in my head, they floated around and kept me up at night. I'd be putting on a shoe, and a storyline would lay itself before me. I would be showering, and a story would lather itself around me. This was so much more rewarding than anything the Coles' offered me, and I promised myself that one day I would pay them back for the education and other luxuries they afforded me and then I would walk away without a thought. I have stopped referring to them as family. They lost rights to that title a long time ago.

Some people didn't understand my anger toward my family. I mean, my parents never abused me, I never wanted for anything but the truth is being me was not enough for them. I was just a smudge on their perfect wall of artwork. They tolerated me because they created me, but if they had a choice, I wouldn't fit in their circle. I was the itch that would not go away. Since I'd moved away, my mother tried to call me every week. I let the phone go to voicemail, and I would later listen to her ramble on about the party she held and how everyone was doing. Melissa extended her partnership, Derrick was traveling again to save another life, and my father was planning to host a gala dinner in aid of yet another cause. I don't delete her voice messages. To be honest, I liked listening to those one-sided conversations on replay when I was alone. Because sometimes her gentle words weighed heavily on my soul and the longing to see my mother's face again was strong. My father has never called, nor have my siblings. I might as well be dead to them.

Growing up Melissa and I were close. We were closer in age than me and Derrick who was six years my senior. Mel and I were inseparable for a long time before the ballet and etiquette lessons kicked in. She wouldn't be seen climbing a tree or throwing a ball around after that. Those were not the kind of things ladies did. With no-one available to talk to or laugh with, I wandered the halls of our manor house, with its imported floor tiles, expensive furniture, and artwork, and felt utterly alone.

Everyone was busy.

Everyone had something to do.

There was no time for Jacob.

"You must learn to fend for yourself boy," my father would grumble.

And so, I did.

Never show them how afraid you are,
Never let them see that they have a hold on you,
Let their darkness come,
The light is already within you.

FOUR
SAGE

I'm cleaning up the table after dinner, a lean chicken breast and rocket salad with no unnecessary dressing. I hated every bite. What I would give for a cheeseburger right now, a juicy, fattening cheeseburger with all the extras. I couldn't remember the last time I had one. Siren sat on the window seat, her elegant legs crossed with an espresso in hand, reading a magazine. She looked up from the magazine and motioned for me to join her. I finished up in the kitchen and approached her cautiously. It was never a good sign for her to summon me. It meant she wanted to *talk* and I could do without her kind of conversations this evening. It had been a busy and emotionally draining day.

"Sit Sage," she ordered. The harsh tone of her voice made me cringe inside. My hands shook, and I wrapped them together to sooth my nerves. I took a seat on the couch across from her and waited for her to acknowledge me. Her attention was on her magazine again and she didn't lift her head up despite knowing I was sitting there expectantly. Instead, she continued to page through it, looking almost content, except I knew better.

"How was your day?" she asked in her casual snobby

tone which told me it's a rhetorical question and she knew everything she needed to know already. It didn't matter that her assumptions were often illogical and misplaced.

"It was a good day Siren, nothing out of the ordinary," I offered cautiously. She considered my answer and shook her head.

"Did anything interesting happen today?"

I sighed. This kind of patronizing was unbearable. "No, Siren, it was just an ordinary, uneventful day at work." I started to wring my hands together nervously, trying not to look at her. She still didn't glance up; her long fingers turned page by page causing me to struggle for breath.

"We do not lie. Do we Sage?" she asked cocking one perfect brow. I nodded knowing that even though she wasn't looking at me, she could see right through me. "Answer me, Sage." She ordered an icy bite of her voice.

"We must not lie, Siren," I said feeling my temples throb. These games exhausted me. I wished that she would just get to the point and say what she wants to say or do what she wants to do. I knew that her silence was too loud. I could feel the tension all through dinner.

She got up and walks towards me rolling the magazine up into a cylinder. It was an Italian Vogue I noticed. She closed the small space between us in seconds.

"Yes Sage," she spat as she stood in front of me tapping the magazine on her thighs. "We must not lie, and yet you do, all the time. Don't you?"

From her tone, I knew that answering her would be futile.

The first hit, although subtle left me dizzy. She picked up speed and intensity and before I knew it I was spluttering and choking as the pain in my head increased. She mumbled something inaudible under her breath. Her blows became more rhythmic. Cold, brutal, and unfeeling, just like her. With every hit I saw the light forming in front of my eyes, and my temples felt like they would explode. Maybe this would be the time she finally killed me. Perhaps I would finally be free from her. My nose started to bleed as she continued her assault to my head. I don't beg for her to stop or plead for her to ease up. It will only make her madder. It was best to take the punishment in silence.

She stopped as suddenly as she started, looking at me out of breath and with anger still burning in her eyes.

"We understand each other then?" she asked, as I cowered on the floor, a bloodied scared mess. She flung the magazine at me, straightened her perfect hair and walked down the hallway disappearing into her bedroom. I could hear her humming as she readied herself for bed. I didn't immediately move or make to get up off the floor. Instead I lay in my blood and saliva and wished for oblivion which I knew would never come.

Siren was calculated.

She wouldn't kill me because she enjoyed my suffering too much.

My head throbbed in agony. I got up slowly and made my way into the kitchen for some water and a painkiller. I wobbled into the bathroom and spent a few minutes cleaning myself up. Surprisingly, there were no bruises on my face. There never were. There cannot be proof of what happened. My head was swollen, I could feel it. I touched the sensitive areas and flinched looking at the ghost staring back at me in the mirror.

What did I ever do to deserve this? Why couldn't I be someone else, even once?

I fetched a bucket and cloth from the laundry room, approaching the living room to clean the area where my blood fell. She must not see the evidence of what happened or be reminded of how angry *I'd* made her. There were many times, she'd told me that she never wanted to do these things to me, but I left her no choice. She'd had to parent me in the absence of our parents growing up, and now I was an inconvenience to her because of my mental state. I was making her life difficult.

Frustrated, I once asked her why she didn't just let me leave. I rushed into my room and packed a suitcase. I didn't make it to the front door. She'd gagged me and left me tied up in the basement storage of our apartment overnight. She was too strong to fight, too strong to resist. I learned my lesson after being hungry and waking up in my mess. I was thirty two-years-old, and yet I lived in fear for my life every single day. I did not have the will or strength to do anything about my situation because in a lot of ways I have brought this upon myself. But lately, the rebel in me has been getting in more trouble than I would like.

I don't know why I do what I sometimes do. I was standing by the office printer all by myself after lunch today when an old woman approached me to ask me if I was okay. I didn't realize how unstable I must have looked wringing my hoodie sleeves.

She was the new office cleaner, and I barely knew her which didn't alert me that she would tell anyone. I didn't think she knew anyone around the building well enough to cause me any trouble. I felt that I could trust her. Her eyes were kind, and she reminded me of someone's grandmother. So I stood there and told her everything. I told her who Siren was, what she's done, and I begged her not to say a word. She'd looked at me with sympathy, took my hand in hers and promised not to say a word to anyone. She told me that I needed to get help. I needed to find the strength and will to fight back because I didn't deserve this kind of treatment.

I trusted her. I trusted a stranger and now I was suffering the repercussions. I knew never to trust anyone but myself. My greatest enemy had told me so.

The first time I'd allowed myself to trust someone I'd been in the fourth grade. I was tired of Siren bullying me all the time and I told my friend Molly Kramer about it. Molly was a nice girl who lived on our street with her grandparents. Unlike me, she wasn't an orphan, but her parents were always traveling, so she spent a lot of time at my house. My grandmother was very fond of her. Molly and I walked to school almost every day. Siren never interacted with people like Molly with her flaming red hair and braces; she was beneath her, she'd pointed that out on more than one occasion.

The friends Siren did have didn't like me. I was not the popular or pretty one. I was the outcast.

"Only losers like you could stomach losers like Molly Kramer." She'd laughed.

I didn't care what Siren thought about Molly, I liked her, and she didn't seem to be interested in being my sister's friend anyway. She would come over and Siren would sunbath outside ignoring us for the entire time that Molly visited. And likewise, Molly and I were comfortable pretending that Siren wasn't even there.

One day on the way to school I told Molly about how Siren bullied me. I told her about the time she'd cut me on my inner arms with my grandfather's Swiss army knife. No-one noticed because they were always hidden by a long sleeve sweater. Molly was horrified. She couldn't believe it.

I tried to convince her but Siren showed up, and everything got a little out of control. I didn't even know that she hadn't left for school yet. She pushed Molly so that my friend fell off the sidewalk and onto the street. Molly scraped her elbow and knee. As she was getting back up, Siren kicked her forcefully in the stomach. She then pulled Molly by the hair and dragged her back onto the pavement. She made her promise not to tell anyone, or she'd throw her in front of a bus. Siren bolted as she usually did; leaving me to deal with the aftermath, which was my job.

Molly nodded, tears streaming down her now dirty face. She stumbled and looked at me in desperation. No, there was something more to her expression. It was fear. She was scared of me. I stood there petrified, unable to speak or breathe. Why would she be scared of me?

I watched Molly disappear down the road. If Molly told on us, there would be hell to pay. My grandparents didn't take kindly to bad behavior. I walked to school and found my sister waiting for me around the corner.

"Why would you do that?" I mumbled.

"Because you never listen to me, you make it seem like I hurt you purposefully. Do you not give me a reason to?"

She walked right up to my face, and I cowered away like a coward. I thought I was her next victim, but she just turned and walked away as if nothing had happened. As if she hadn't just threatened a girl, my friend, with death.

Siren was more messed up than I realized.

FIVE
JAKE

The office building was entirely glass and steel, large and overpowering. It towered over the small business district, a leader amongst the followers and I would be working here. I walked up the staircase towards the large revolving doors. Walking into the foyer was even more impressive than the exterior. The glass and steel design carried in from the outside and in the foyer, you could see so far up it felt like you could see every floor, all twenty of them spiraled up and above you. This was true architecture. I marveled at the lighting and interior design. Couches were scattered around, the contemporary décor fitting perfectly. The meeting rooms were to the left. I was stunned at the fact that just a month ago; I sat on one of those couches anxiously awaiting my interview for this position.

I walked over to the large reception desk and was greeted by a chirpy blonde woman about my age. She was the epitome of the *face* of an organization. She stood up to greet me with a smile on her heart-shaped face, and I couldn't help but notice how her uniform fit perfectly on her curvaceous frame. She was tall, about 5 feet to my 6. She looked like she belonged on a catwalk. I shouldn't say that out loud though.

"Hi, Jake Cole, I'm here to see Mr. Hart," I confidently offered her my hand in greeting. She took it. "It's my first day," I grinned, kicking myself for that dumb line.

"Well welcome to Sky Corp, Mr. Cole, I'm Paula, and we're certainly glad to have you," she winked.

"Just Jake," I said, offering her a wink of my own which caused her to flush.

She picked up the phone in front of her and dialed who I assumed was Mr. Hart, without breaking eye contact. The Cole effect.

"Well, Just Jake, take the elevator up to the 4th floor, and I am sure someone will be there to greet you," she leaned over the counter and twirled a finger around her curls. "And if you ever need a tour, I'd be happy to show you around." I doubted that was all she'd be showing me.

"Thank you, Paula," I cleared my throat. I have never been a blonde kind of guy. I preferred my woman dark and exotic, but for Miss Paula, I could make an exception. I smiled as I entered the impressive glass elevator and took the short ride up to the 4th floor. This was going to be interesting.

I stepped out into a small dusty foyer with an oversized pot plant which was positioned almost directly in front of the elevator door. I took in the musty smell, and I knew I was home. I took a deep breath, smelling the paper, old books and - something sweet? Where did that come from?

"Mr. Cole?" asked a small voice from behind me. I turned around quickly. I hadn't even noticed her standing there when I got off the elevator. She was so small she was probably standing behind the plant all along.

"I-I'm Sage Fenton, and uhm Steve, Mr. Hart, asked me to welcome you," she whispered. I could tell she was extremely nervous by the way she kept shifting on her feet.

She's a tiny thing, about 4 feet. She's in skinny jeans and an oversized gray hoodie with the words Platform 9 and $^{3}/_{4 \text{ on}}$ it, a Harry Potter Fan. Something we have in common. I can't see much of her face, just her black hair that hung through the hood which was pulled down. Her skin was pale. She wore Chuck Taylors, and I assumed she's a volunteer from high school. Either that or one inappropriately dressed professional. Her voice though caught me off guard. She's a lot older.

"Thank you, Sage," I offered her my hands only to have her stick hers in her pockets.

"Follow me," she brushed past me and led me through an array of cubicles overrun with paper until we reached a small corner office. Everyone had their heads buried in a stack of paper, others were typing away on their desktop computers. Nobody paid much attention as I followed Sage down the passage and we came to a stop outside an office.

"Come in Cole, shut the door behind you!" bellowed a burly man in his mid-forties. "You can leave now Sage," he dismissed the girl-like woman without fully acknowledging her.

"Hi Mr. Hart, it is such a pleasure to see you again," I offered him a hand he didn't take. People weren't all that friendly here.

"It's Steve, sit," he growled. "Let me get a few things straight, you're here to work, Cole, do as you're told, keep your nose clean and you'll be alright. Take the office next to mine, if you need anything ask Sage. She's a bit quiet, but she knows what she's doing."

If he weren't so dismissive and hard, I would swear he cared for Sage. I doubted that. This man didn't seem to care about much at all. He stared at his desk which I assumed was an indication that our conversation was over.

"Thank you, Steve," I get up to leave. He continued to stare down at some paperwork on his desk completely ignoring me.

I entered the small office next door, and it's a simple setup, desk, chair, telephone, and a bookshelf. I thought Steve's office was small but this one was miniature in comparison. It had a window, but the only view was of the side of another building and scaffolding. There's a box on my desk which I assumed was full of manuscripts. Talk about hitting the ground running. I grinned. I loved it. I loved it all. I placed my bag down on the visitor's chair. I sat down and took in the smells and textures of my new office. I smiled, taking a manuscript from the pile.

An hour in I decided to take a walk around the floor and maybe find out where I can get some decent coffee to start my day. There were a few people working on this floor, the team including Steve and myself were about ten. I greeted everyone and made small talk. They all seemed courteous but in a hurry to get back to work. When I arrived at Sage's cubicle, I found her staring out of the window. I watched her for a few seconds wondering what about the wall of the building had caught her interest, and knocked on the cubicle wall so as not to startle her. She was startled anyway.

"Can I help you Mr. Cole?" she asked hesitantly, her eyes downcast.

"You can call me Jake, just Jake, Sage," I tell her.

"Jake," she seemed to consider the name, and it sounded good from those lips in that fragrant voice.

When she spoke, I imagined the angels in heaven compiling a symphony specific for each word she uttered. She sang her words, instead of speaking them. I shook my head. I was losing it.

"No, I was just getting to know everyone and what they do around here," I inform her, hoping she'll speak again. I tried to see more of her face but it's no use; she was looking down again and fiddling with the papers on her desk.

"I do any work you and Steve ask me to, copies, filing, posting of manuscripts, receiving them, setting up appointments, that kind of thing," she sang in that mesmerizing voice. She could have been asking me to give up my soul, and I would gladly oblige.

"Great, thanks for letting me know Sage," I cleared my throat not wanting to come across as creepy. What on earth is wrong with me? I can barely see the girls face, for all I know she's downright hideous under all that hair and hoodie. I doubted that though. Even though she kept her eyes downcast and did her best not to look me in the eyes, I knew that there was something special about Sage Fenton.

"Do you have any idea where I can get some coffee in this joint?"

"There's a coffee machine on the third floor we all use, that and the staff restaurant on the ground floor."

"Thank you, Sage." I turned around and headed back to my office. I'll have coffee later. I'd better get cracking on that box.

I want to be consumed by this darkness,
Ride away with it into the night,
Feel it caress my skin,
Let it take over my soul,
I want to kiss it with my last breath,
Linger with it just a moment longer,
I want it to engulf me,
take me,
own me,
I want to lose myself in this darkness that is you.

SIX
SAGE

She's in an exceptionally taunting mood tonight, and I wondered if she had a bad day at the office. I wanted to ask her about it, but I don't. I wanted to have these kinds of normal conversations with my sister, but that was asking for the impossible. I couldn't remember a time when we just sat together and spoke about our day, about lives, about our aspirations. Every day was like walking into a battlefield with her.

"You should do more around here, Sage; this place is a fucking pig sty." She shouted causing me to tense up.

"I will Siren, just tell me what to do and I will," I respond helplessly. I don't know how to please her. I do everything anyway. I have done so, our whole lives, but it is never enough. The place was spotless. There was no doubt about that. I made sure of it every single day, but she still scoffed and belittled me. Nothing I ever did would ever satisfy her. I didn't know why I even bothered. I reminded myself that I didn't have a choice.

"You're so dumb Sage, it's no wonder you're working in such a pathetic job. You're lucky anyone hired you at all," she usually berated, her perfect nose in the air.

The funny thing was she was right. I'd always been

inferior to Siren at everything, academically growing up and now professionally. On the other hand, there was one thing that was mine and mine alone, my writing. And she did everything she possibly could to stop me from doing anything about it. She let me read but no time could be spent on writing, except when she went to bed. I had all those hours to myself, and I utilized it well. I didn't need more than three hours of sleep anyway.

A crashing sound startled me. I looked down to find that a plate she had flung across the table had landed close enough that small shards of glass were stuck to my ankles. A shiver ran through me.

"I told you to get out of that head of yours Sage, how dare you not listen to me," she snarled.

"I'm sorry Siren, I have a headache, I'm sorry," I responded, as honestly as I could muster.

"You always have excuses! Just clean up and make it quick, we're going out tonight." She got up and stormed out of the room.

I breathe a sigh of relief. It's unbelievable sometimes that we are sisters and that she treats me as awful as she does. I knew about spouses who physically, mentally and emotionally abused each other but I didn't know that someone as close to me as my sister could do this. I should be running to her for protection from the world outside; instead, the monster lived within these four walls, and I had no way to get away from it.

I hated going out with Siren, she always took us to nightclubs, and I hated those. I just wanted to be at home. It was Friday night, and I was exhausted from a busy week. But I didn't have a choice. I cleaned up as fast as I could and got dressed. She didn't approve of anything I wore so I stuck to my skinny jeans, threw on a pair of short heeled Timberlands and an off shoulder beige blouse. She never allowed me to wear a hoodie when we went out. I left my hair loose, and it fell down my back. I was not that bad to look at, was I? Surely being Siren's twin meant something.

I exited the room at the same time she did and she cocked an eyebrow at me. "You don't look half bad tonight," I can't help but feel that she's disappointed about that too.

She wore a glittering red dress and a pair of killer black pumps with a red heel. Her hair was hooked up on one end and the rest of it fell over her shoulder. She wore blood red lipstick, and her eyelashes were even longer than usual because of mascara. She was dressed to kill, and I felt unworthy standing next to her.

"Head down at all times Sage. I will not say that again, "she chanted. We hopped into her car, and she sped down the highway into the busiest part of town, where the nightlife happened.

I sat calmly, my hands in my lap, trying to breathe. These outing never went well for me. There was the time a guy approached me for a dance. I was chastised for my insolence despite the fact that I declined. How was it possible not to talk to people in a place like a club? How can I sit in a corner and not respond to the people that are always approaching me? How do I be the recluse she wants me to be when the environment doesn't allow me to?

We walked into the dimly lit, overcrowded nightclub that we usually frequent. Smoke fills the air from the smoke machines and hookah pipes. There was a stage, which I assumed was for the evening's entertainment. The music was blaring, and I had to resist the urge to block my ears. Sweaty bodies, scantily clad, clammed together on the dance floor. Everyone was intoxicated and having the time of their lives. I envied them; I wished that I could let my hair down and be free like them. Euphoria was written all over their faces, and I craved that. Siren found us a table in the corner, and we sat down. She ordered us a few drinks, and as was usually the case, she left me behind to lose herself on the dance floor. I watched her, everyone watched her, and all eyes were on her. She moved her body sensually, and I stared at her in wonder. What was it like to have the world at your feet? The crowd edged closer to her, as if in a trance. She was like a spider, dangerously attracting those helpless fools to her, only to have them caught in her silken web before she pounced and sucked the life from them in much the same way that she's done to me. I needed a stronger poison. But nothing seemed to relieve me from my misery these days. I got up and made my way to the bar hoping to get lost, even for a little while.

SEVEN

JAKE

I thought I might be mistaken at first, but I wasn't. She didn't have her hoodie on, and I could see more of her face, not much because she faced away from me, but I made out that she had high cheekbones and large eyes with pretty eyelashes. Her dark hair was long and styled. She kept blinking in rhythm. She spoke to the bartender, and I knew it's her. She had subtle lips that looked soft enough to the touch. I would like to taste them. I frowned at the direction of my thought. In my moment of confusion, she turned towards me, and her eyes grew large as she took me in. She was frighteningly and hauntingly beautiful; her eyes were the color of black tourmaline, dark and sad. She had the kind of eyes you could lose yourself in. She hurriedly turned away, no doubt hoping I hadn't seen her. I smiled at that and made my way over to her.

I took the seat next to her. "Hi Sage," I smiled. She turned to me, and she was even more breathtaking up close. I was not usually this taken by a woman. Although in all honesty, I haven't dated anyone for a long time. The last socialite I dated was a friend of my sisters and couldn't handle my apparent lack of interest in the Cole name and fortune.

"Hi, Jake," she responded nervously. She pulled her hair over her shoulders and sunk into herself as if to hide from me.

"I didn't peg you for the club scene type," I grinned.

She smiled at me nervously. It's a beautiful smile, and I wondered why a gorgeous woman like her didn't use that smile more often.

"I didn't peg you for the judging type," she taunted, cocking one elegant eyebrow.

I laughed. She had a point.

"Point taken," I threw my hands up in mock surrender.

"Can I buy you a drink, Sage?" I motioned to her half empty glass. She traced her fingers on the rim. If it weren't so rowdy in here, it would emit a sound I find fascinating.

"No thanks, I've just ordered." The bartender walked over to us, just as I was about to throw a cocky retort.

"Are you here alone?" I asked. I can't help but lean in closer. There it was again, that sweet scent. Honey and vanilla.

"You?" she teased, evading my question. She doesn't move away. Instead, she finally met my gaze, and for a second, I seemed to forget how to respond.

"Yes, actually, new in town and all that," I grin. She smiled again, and I knew that if she didn't stop doing that, I'd do or say something I would later kick myself for.

"You want to dance Sage?" I leaned in to whisper in her ear, inhaling her sweet scent.

She's about to answer me when she glances over her shoulder and the panic starts to set in. I see it in the darting of her eyes and the heaving of her chest.

"I'm sorry, I can't. But thank you," she stuttered, abruptly getting up to leave.

I tried to reach for her arm, but she shrugged me off. I can't help but feel that she's afraid of something or someone. I turn around, but no-one seems to be paying attention to us at the bar, everyone is dancing and having a good time. I shouldn't have done that. Why did I do that? I just met this girl recently and she was obviously not into socializing. I felt like such a fool as I watched her walk away into the crowd. Her dark hair flowed behind her. She doesn't look back. I was just trying to be friendly. I ordered a beer and looked around.

"Don't worry about her, she's weird like that," a woman, who sounded oddly familiar, offered from behind me. I turned around to find her leaning against the bar on the other side of me. "There are plenty of us who would like to dance," she purred. I doubted that dancing is all that's on her mind.

"Paula? Hi," I smirked, actually glad to see her. I needed to get my mind off Sage and the fact that I don't know a damn thing about her and she's suddenly occupying my thoughts, causing me to act completely out of character. Paula looked stunning in an electric blue dress, her blonde hair in a high ponytail.

"Hi, Just Jake," she giggled.

"It's good to see you again," I motioned for the bartender in the hopes of starting a very interesting night.

"Can I get you a drink?"

"I'd love a Long Island Ice Tea," she smiled. She took the seat next to me, leaning on me slightly. Our drinks arrived, and we chatted and drank. Later we made our way to the dance floor; all thoughts of Sage and her haunting beauty were long forgotten.

EIGHT

SAGE

His tousled brown hair fell over his eyes when he concentrated, and he had a dimple on his right cheek when he smiled. He had light brown eyes that almost matched his hair. He had a strong jaw and a short beard which others might mistake for stubble, but I knew that it was just his look. He walked around with confidence and purpose, and unlike me, his head was never down. He's gorgeous.

There was no doubt about that. His shirts hugged him just right, the sleeves were rolled up to display his arms which were tanned and toned. His pants hung in a way that made you imagine what might be hidden under all that. He was tall and had quite a few inches on me. He was someone I could write about someday. He'd make one sexy book boyfriend.

I smiled. Jake Cole could be the hero of my story any day. I didn't know why I'd been noticing those things about Jake, but I did which was not surprising, seeing as I have been observing people for most of my life. It's what I do best, watch and learn how *normal* people should act and interact, people who aren't controlled by a sadistic sister.

I can say these things to myself because she doesn't know. If I don't say them out loud where someone can overhear them, she will not find out about it. I don't know why I let her do these things to me, but I suppose I have no-one else and nowhere else to go. My grandmother doesn't want anything to do with either of us. After we left town, she made it clear that her home would never be open to us.

I lived by Sirens rules now. We lived in her choice of apartment. I do as she says. Our joint savings account was controlled by Siren. I don't even have a driver's license because she felt I didn't need one and I didn't have the energy to fight her on it. I was tired of fighting. What good would that do me?

Jake hadn't spoken to me frankly since his first day at the office, except if it related to work. I guess I preferred it that way. It kept me out of trouble. He was very good at his job, I could tell. I'd been working here long enough. Steve hadn't thrown a manuscript out of his window as yet when Jake presented it.

But seeing him at the club tonight, seeing him relaxed, extremely good looking and flirtatious, left me reeling. His personality drew me in, and despite my reservations and fears, I smiled at him and even attempted to flirt. But maybe I imagined the flirting. I have not been hit on for a long time. That was more up Siren's alley. She was the sexy, likable sister and I was not.

I saw Siren out of the corner of my eye as she exited the ladies room. I didn't think that she could see me clearly from where she stood, but I couldn't be sure.

"I have to go," I abruptly halted our conversation.

"But I just got here, stay a little while." he pleaded.

"I — I can't. Bye Jake. "I quickly left Jake with no explanation.

But what if she saw the exchange at the bar? What if she overheard him offering me a drink and thought I'd initiated the conversation?

She stalked up to me.

"We're leaving!" she stated.

I followed her out without saying a word, and I knew she knew everything the moment we got into the car. She sped off without even looking in my direction. I just sat there a little bit frazzled.

"I didn't say anything to him," I start hoping that if I set that straight, she'd understand. "He's my new boss Siren. I couldn't just sit there saying nothing. That would be insane."

"You are not to speak to people, Sage, except if it is absolutely necessary, you're not supposed to get friendly, you're supposed to keep your head down at all times. Do you want to destroy my life, Sage? Is that what you want? You ungrateful little…"

I wondered how *me* talking to someone she doesn't even know will destroy *her* life but I don't try to rationalize that. No there was no reasoning with Siren. She is always right.

"No Siren, I wouldn't do that, I'm sorry, I wasn't thinking. I will never do it again, not again." I started to sob, and my head started to ache.

She sped up, and we had to be going a few miles

above the speed limit because I felt like my insides were wobbling all over the place. She drives recklessly when she's mad and especially after she's had a few drinks. She doesn't care about the consequences. She suddenly pulls off on the side of the road. She's breathing heavily. She glared at me, and I know I was going to hate whatever it is she has decided to do. She gets out and comes around to my side of the car and opens my door. The wind hits me, and I heard the cars whizzing past us, it's a busy highway. Every now and then our car shifts because of the movement, and it causes my insides to clench.

"No Siren, please," I begged not knowing what she would do to me. I knew I had to try and get through to her. I have not defied her. I have done nothing that deserved any of what she planned to do.

"You make me do these things Sage, you make me punish you, you're always so pathetic and unworthy, and I tolerate you because you're my sister." She snarled. She's close to hysterics now, her eyes darting around manically. All traces of sanity and rational thinking have left her.

"Do you know the sacrifices I make every single day, for you, for us? Do you not know that I love you, that I want to protect you?" she chided. "And yet, you defy me every chance you get.

I sat shivering and sobbing afraid that I may have pushed her too far this time.

She straightened her back, a woman on a mission, her black coat flapping in the wind, her hair whirling around her. She twisted her face into an ugly scowl, and I knew I was going to suffer. A shiver ran down my spine.

I let the tears fall, not caring that she called crying an illness and weakness. Whatever this woman was going to do to me was worthy of these tears. I knew that.

"Place your hands here, Sage, and don't even try to move," she roughly positioned my hands around the door frame. She wouldn't do something so cruel, would she? "You're a selfish little bitch Sage, remember that," she growled.

When she slammed the door against my hand the first time, a wail escaped me. It hurt so much. I couldn't breathe. I barely had time to recover when she slammed it again. She slammed it until the pain was replaced by numbness. When she stopped, my hands looked mauled and broken. She dragged my broken hand roughly into my lap. I shivered in pain and disbelief. She slammed the door shut so hard I flinched. She got behind the wheel and checked her hair in the rearview mirror as if nothing had happened. The pain stunned me into silence. I can't look at her. I just looked ahead at the road in front of me.

"Are you sorry Sage?" she taunted, placing her hand roughly on my injured hand and sneering, obviously pleased with the sight of my hand.

"I am, Siren, I'm sorry," I croaked, knowing that I must answer her.

We made our way to the hospital in silence, where she would sit in the car outside as she usually did, while I went into the emergency unit and made up an excuse about how I'd gotten injured. I wasn't sure how to explain this. All I knew was that she would be waiting for me and if I dared make one false move, she would hurt me again and I didn't know if I could survive any more punishment today. She could have me sent away again, and I don't think I could survive that. No, I had to get the treatment I needed and then forget that this incident happened. That was the only way that I would survive.

NINE

JAKE

She wasn't at work for a whole week after I saw her at the club and when she did return, she had a cast on one wrist. I wondered what happened to her, but I dared not ask. Steve warned me to leave her be, and I did just that. She wore her hoodie again, and she got straight to work. Steve allocated her the jobs that she could manage with one hand, and I could tell that she was frustrated. I didn't know why I wanted to talk to her so much, but I knew I shouldn't. She was obviously the way she was for a reason. I hoped that the hand didn't hurt too much. I'd broken my wrist ice-skating once, and I was flat lined for a few weeks after that in excruciating pain. My father hated whiners, so my nanny took care of me in the guest house. I was six at the time.

The office was empty, just Sage and me. She always worked late and today was no exception. I'd settled in well, thanks to her. I appreciated the freedom this job gave me. I enjoyed the places it took me through the pages of the various manuscripts I read. Entering the mind of one writer after another and getting a glimpse of their souls on paper. That was what it was to me, a tendering of souls. I watched her through my open door and hoped that she would talk to me with no-one around. I didn't want to scare her off, but she was a colleague, and it was only normal to feel concerned about her. I wondered if she was in an abusive relationship. She displayed all the signs. She was edgy, nervous and anti-social, afraid to look or talk to anyone and now her injury. I shut the manuscript I was working on, and when I finally work up the nerve to approach her, I spot Paula walking down the passage.

"Hey handsome," she smiled as she approached me, her handbag in hand and coat slung over her arm. She stands on her tiptoes and plants a kiss me on my lips. Office romances are officially the worst. Her perfume was overly strong this evening. Her tight work shirt had a button loose which I didn't doubt for a second was done intentionally.

"Hey, what are you doing here so late?" We started this sort of friends with benefits arrangement since that night at the club, but she knew that was all I wanted right now. I have never been someone who was after commitment and romance, not after growing up in the Cole household and my recent gold digger fiasco. I'd made that clear to her, well I hoped I had. Because it didn't explain the angry girlfriend stance she suddenly took.

"You, Me, Dinner, remember?" She motioned between us frowning.

Shit. I forgot that I agreed we could have dinner tonight. Well, that was before the urgent manuscript came in.

"I'm sorry Paula, no can do, something urgent came up, and I've got to burn the midnight oil," I motioned to my desk, stacked high with papers.

She leaned into me and pushed her impressive cleavage into my chest.

"I can make it worth your while," she whispered.

"As tempting as that sounds, I've got to get this done," I said regrettably. "I'm sorry," I planted a chaste kiss on her cheek.

She nods, obviously disappointed and turned around to leave. She sauntered down the passage and threw Sage a disgusted glance.

I shook my head and decide that talking to Sage after she heard all that was not something I could do. I closed myself in my office and dove into an enthralling manuscript. One I knew would be a bestseller just by the prologue.

A knock on the door startled me, and I looked at the time. It was past nine.

"I'm leaving for the day, Mr. Cole," Sage announced.

"Just Jake, Sage," I smiled.

"Jake," she corrected.

"Are you getting home alright," I queried. "It's pretty late."

"I'll be okay thanks. Anyway, I'll see you tomorrow."

"Sage, are – are you okay, the wrist I mean," I motioned to her arm.

"I am fine thanks, Jake," she smiled but I could tell that she didn't mean it.

Still, I don't push her, whatever it was I know this girl

has to deal with it on her own. She doesn't take too kindly to forging friendships.

"Good night, Sage," I start, but she's already started to walk away.

I go back to my manuscript, but I can't get that beautifully haunted face off my mind. The way she looked that night has been at the forefront of my mind. I go to sleep at night, and I see those dark orbs staring back at me. I don't know what it is about her that intrigues me. It could be the fact that there is no woman I have ever met that hasn't fallen for my charm and well, good looks.

I raked my hands through my much in need of a haircut hair and continued reading.

TEN

SAGE

Things have been unnervingly quiet at home. I didn't argue with Siren about anything, and I didn't act in a way that would anger her. We ate dinner on time, and she usually retreated to her cave and me to mine. I'd taken to sneaking a bottle of whiskey into my room now and then. I would sit on the carpet taking long swigs from the bottle. It helped ease the tension. I hide it behind the bookshelf in my secret place which she doesn't seem to know or care about, along with my manuscript and other things. It was just a hole I dug in the wall over time when she was in the bath or asleep. She often tells me that I am not a prisoner that I am free to come and go as I please but that was laughable because whenever I did try to go out she would make my life a living hell.

But within these walls I was free. What she doesn't know won't hurt me, I think to myself at night. Tonight was exceptionally quiet. She barely spoke two words to me since we walked through the door. At first, I thought she was angry, but I couldn't remember doing anything wrong, but on closer observation, I noticed the faintest hint of nervousness. I didn't know what it was or what it meant, but it was there. I knew this because I knew people. I noticed the occasional sighs and glances my way at dinner. The way her hands slightly trembled as she held her cutlery and the way she took a deep breath now and then.

Tonight I feel stronger somehow. I took a long swig from my bottle of whiskey and remind myself to replenish my stash soon. I'm nearly done with my story. It's more like a full-length novel now, and when I'm done, maybe I will submit to Steve, and he can tell me what he thinks about it. These thoughts scare me even more than Siren does. I know I have to keep it a secret but I wished so much that I could share it with someone. Why couldn't Siren and I have a normal relationship? We barely talk to each other except if she wants to insult me. Sometimes I think of talking to her, about everything and begging that we start over, but I know that I don't have any right to do that. My rights were taken away from me as she often reminded me. She's warned me about Jake, warned me that if I dared speak to him again, she would make sure we both suffered, like the last time.

Anyone who ever hears my story may wonder why I am so weak. Why can't I just fight her back? She's a human being after all. But no-one will understand her true power. I take another drink. I don't want to think about that, but I can't help when the memories come flooding back. I curled into a ball, and I wept in silence.

ELEVEN

SAGE

"I think I love him, Siren," I said to her happily. She sat on the lounger, reading a book, something dark and dangerous, and the epitome of Siren. She doesn't read, but when she does, you can bet it's something that messed with the mind. Gathering tips, I suppose.

She looked up at me and cocked an eyebrow.

"And what would you know about love at 18, Sage?" she scoffed.

"A lot more than you do," I stormed off not wanting to have yet another conversation where she belittled me, and I let her.

A few hours later, I looked up from my bed to find her leaning against the doorframe. She wore simple blue jeans and a button-down shirt, her hair in a high ponytail, but she still looked like she stepped off a movie set. How does she do that?

"He will never love you, Sage," she sneered.

"He does love me Siren," I demand with surety. I sat up and glared at her. "Why can't you just be happy for me Siren, even just this once," I whispered, the tears threatened to fall. No, I must not show weakness, that was what she fed off.

"I cannot be happy for you because *you* do not deserve to be happy Sage. Happiness has never been in the cards for you." She laughed.

"How can you even say that?" I looked at her in disbelief. "You're my sister!"

"I said it because it's true." She stated matter-of-factly.

"You're just jealous that someone is interested in me because no-one can handle your slimy attitude," I bit back.

"Happiness is just a daydream Sage, and I will prove it to you," she sneered walking away.

I fell back on the bed, exhausted. I am always exhausted after a conversation with Siren.

I knew Dale loves me. He told me so several times. Dale and I met a year ago and our time together has been nothing less than perfect. We have plans to leave the country when we graduate, travel to London maybe. He, the struggling musician and me, the writer, it would be wonderful. I just had to get the hell away from Siren. This whole control thing she holds over me must end. We are sisters, equals.

I must have dozed off because I woke up to insistent pounding on our apartment door.

"Siren! Get the door!" I shout, but she doesn't respond. She must be out like she usually is after we fight.

I got up, and my head hurt, my hands hurt too and I felt like I'd been hit by a truck.

I slowly made my way to the front door opening it, yawning.

I'm surprised to see a policewoman at the door.

"Hello," I offered, uncertain why the police would be at our apartment.

"Ms. Sage Fenton?" asked the uniformed policewoman at the door.

"Yes? Is everything okay?" My blood ran cold thinking that Siren must be in some trouble. My sister can be cruel, but I would never want anything to happen to her.

"Ms. Fenton you are being placed under arrest for the alleged assault and attempted murder of one Mr. Dale Evans, you have the right to remain silent. Anything you say can and will be used against you in a court of law. You have the right to speak to an attorney, and to have an attorney present during any questioning. If you cannot afford a lawyer, one will be provided for you at government expense."

"Dale?" I whispered. Her words play back in my mind. "What, no this is a mistake!" I shouted. "Siren, they're making a mistake!" I hoped she'd hear me and rescue me but she was nowhere to be seen. "I would never hurt Dale, never, I love him." I tried to convince the severe looking policewoman.

"Ms. Fenton, I would advise you not to say anything further until you have a lawyer," the woman advised as she reached behind me, turned me around gently and cuffed me. I looked down, and it was then that I noticed the blood stains on my shirt and jeans. What, that wasn't there when I went to sleep earlier. This was a mistake. Oh, God. Was Dale okay?

"No," I struggled against the restraints. "Is Dale okay?" I questioned.

"Ms. Fenton, I suggest you come with us calmly," the other police officer added.

"No!" I shouted but hung my head knowing that it was no use fighting this. I just needed to go with the flow and see how this played out. The tears streamed down my face as they led me down the crowded hallway and outside my building. My neighbors watched in horror as the scene unfolded in front of them. I imagined all the incorrect assumptions they were making right now.

At the police station, I was placed in a small, dirty holding room. The walls, ceiling, and tiles had seen better days. A wooden desk and two chairs were the only furniture in the room. The desk had several carvings in it. The chairs are the uncomfortable kind I used to have in high school. I imagined the real disgusting criminals who have sat in this very chair, and I wanted to hurl. How could they put me in the same category as those monsters?

I'm eighteen years old and I sure as hell wouldn't hurt anyone, least of all the love of my life. The room had a solid iron door with a small square glass window. I could see uniformed officers and civilians walking by. They were free, unlike me.

This has been my home for the last few hours. I thought about my grandparents and how disappointed they would be if they heard about this. Siren wouldn't miss a chance to inform them of what a failure I was, although she didn't bother with them much lately.

I couldn't understand how Siren could be so cold hearted and remorseful. Our grandparents weren't the best but they were good enough to us both, treating us kindly. They weren't our parents, and there were times when we wished to be anywhere else, but we were okay, we had everything we needed. They did everything they possibly could for us and yet she always found a way to be ungrateful and spiteful. Doing unthinkable things and blaming me for it. There was the one time she burnt the curtains which were hanging in their home since they moved into that house. She would sell their ornaments and jewelry for pot money and once, she set alight their wedding album.

I remembered our grandmother crying for days after the wedding album incident. When we were older Siren would steal their money and buy drugs with it, planting it in my dressing table or under my mattress where she knew they would find it. They cared for us both, but Siren had a special place in their hearts, I knew this because she never got in trouble. No matter what she did and as we grew older, I just took the heat. She was the golden child, and I would always be blamed.

As if on cue she walked into the room. She sported her favorite pair of jeans, a jersey top, and heels. She looked amazing and well-kempt as always. She placed a tissue on the chair opposite me and sat down haughtily, folding her slender legs in front of her. "Tsk, Tsk, Tsk, Sage, Sage, Sage, what the fuck have you gotten yourself into?"

"How did you even get in here Siren?" I growled.

"I have friends everywhere Sage," she said sweetly turning to wink at the officer outside the door.

"I didn't do anything Siren, I was at home the whole afternoon, and you know it," I spat.

"I've been out all day Sage. How would I know that?" she asked checking her newly painted nails. "I hear they have footage of you losing control and beating the living daylights out of poor Dale Evans. You hit him from behind with a fire extinguisher first and then bashed him senseless when he was on the floor." She mocked a horrified expression. "You're heartless Sage, cruel." she faked a cry grabbing a tissue from her bag for theatrics.

I knew all of that. I'd heard it all. I'd been grilled by the detectives to the point of laughter after I couldn't cry anymore. I couldn't understand any of it. How could I not remember doing any of what they'd accused me of? What motive did I have? I loved Dale, and he loved me. I hadn't even seen him today. I'd messaged him, but suddenly it dawned on me.

Happiness is just a daydream Sage and I will prove it to you.

Those contaminated, hate-filled words came to me, and I broke down and cried.

"Why Siren, why would you do this to me?" I asked her helplessly.

"Because you never listen," she answered plainly while reapplying her lipstick. She never needed a hand mirror. She'd once sneered that my glassy tear-filled eyes were always the clearest mirror.

"You're always trying to work against me, against the plan I have for you, for us," she taunted.

"What plan Siren, to keep me your prisoner forever, to taunt and control me, to refuse me the dignity of my own decisions? I sobbed.

"You're getting it all wrong Sage," she soothed getting up to cross the room. "I am protecting you."

"You remember Molly don't you? You remember how our grandparents didn't believe it was me?"

"You remember how people turned against you and hurt you. I have been the only one who has been good to you Sage, *ME* and now you insult me with your delusions."

"They aren't delusions Siren," I said through gritted teeth.

She undoes the scarf around her neck and gags me with it spinning my chair around. I can't breathe. She gripped my head with one hand and slammed my head back onto the metal table. The pain was blinding. I couldn't scream, and I felt the tears running down my cheeks and pooling in my ears.

The room started to spin when she slammed me into

the table again.

"It's going to get worse Sage, so much worse but I can make this all go away." She hissed in my ear.

"I can make all of the allegations disappear."

I shook my head, refusing to allow her to manipulate me anymore. I won't do it. I would rather die.

She slammed my head into the table once more, and the pain caused me to piss myself.

I caved. I nodded. I nodded so hard it hurts.

Temporarily insane that was the term they used to define me. My grandparents came to the station and gave their statement and left. They didn't wait to see me. Since it was my first offense, I was lucky. I had to spend some time doing community service. Dale eventually dropped the charges, so I didn't have to worry about a criminal record.

He did however; demand that I never come near him. He never wanted to see me again. The thought of what I'd put him through shattered me. I cried myself to sleep almost every night but all that mattered was that I was free, well in one sense, but Siren never let me forget what she'd *done* for me or what she could do if I didn't toe the line.

I was to remain quiet, let her make all the rules and keep my head down. I was an inconvenience, and she always reminded me of it. I thought of taking my own life and even attempted it a few but she always managed to get there in time, and the penance of such an act was severe.

Eventually I realized that sometimes you had to give up your own free will for the sake of survival.

TWELVE
JAKE

I couldn't get her off my mind. I tried. Fuck I tried but I just couldn't. I felt like a teenager with a crush on the cutest girl in school, but she didn't even know I existed. Maybe it was the chase. Maybe that was what drew me to her. Whatever it was I had to know more about her.

Paula and I were out for dinner, and as usual, my mind wandered to Sage. Paula was pretty and cool, and sometimes I felt like she understood this thing between us, but there were other times, like right now, when she looked at me like she's expecting more. I could like someone like Paula, but she didn't give me those *feels* deep down. She seemed like the clingy type, the "Touch my man, and I'll skin you alive" kind. That isn't such a bad thing, but I preferred subtlety sometimes. A woman who can stake her claim and have no questions asked a woman who can delve into the soul of man and leave him reeling, an intellectual woman that I could share my innermost thoughts with. Despite what women think or how they behave around me, I'm not a bad boy or heartbreaker, just a man that likes to have fun until I find the one I am looking for and when that search is over, it's over.

"Where are you when you're not here?" she tapped

my temple.

"Just work stuff, nothing important." I lied. I was also not the kind of man that was going to bear his soul to a woman like Paula. I know why she sticks around, despite my own reluctance to make things official with her. I saw her on Google, researching my family. She thought I was asleep, but I wasn't. I ignored it because I didn't care. It just let me see right through her, and that was a good thing. People knew the Cole's. They were the elite of the elite, in every social circle, and I was one of them, or, well I used to be. Strike one. I knew her type.

"So I was wondering if you wanted to go to the nightclub after this. Just for a short while to relax, listen to some good music, and have a few drinks and then we can go over to your place for a private party. She swirled her long hair around her finger.

Oh fuck, she knew the rules. Strike two.

"I mean my place," she corrected, but I don't miss the disappointment. But I have to admit that after a dinner like the one I just sat through, a drink sounded perfect.

"Yeah sure, shall we go then," I frowned. She didn't seem to notice my annoyance and signaled over a waiter. I shook my head and asked for the bill.

I was at the bar getting Paula and I drinks when I spot her. At first, I think I'm hallucinating but sure as hell it's Sage and she's – is she dancing? She seemed to be in a trance. I watched her, mesmerized, unable to take my eyes off her. This wasn't the Sage I knew at all. The last time I met her, she was so much less – well sexy. She was beautiful yes, but the woman on the dance floor oozed sex appeal. She wore a gold fitted mini-dress and matching heels; her long hair was loose and fell down her back. She ran her hand through her hair, and she proceeded to run her hands all the way down her face and when she cupped her breasts I gulped. What the fuck is she doing? She was a sight to behold in this smoke-filled room. I watched the crowd as they gathered around, they watch her, but none of them moved toward her, she had them in a trance. The music slowed, and she swayed her hips to the rhythm. I met her gaze across the room, and she smiled at me biting her bottom lip. She beckoned me with a finger, and I wanted to go over there, but I was holding drinks. I looked down at my hands, and when I looked up again, she was gone. Man, I am losing it. That couldn't have been her.

The thoughts of her left me restless. Women don't have that effect on me. I usually do this to them. I looked over at Paula.

"I want to leave," I growled.

"But we just got here," she sulked.

"I want to fuck, Paula, now!" I demanded.

We don't make it to the car. I practically carry her to the dark side of the building, and after slipping on a condom, I take her against the wall. Her legs curled against my waist as I held her weight up. With every thrust I was reminded that this was all this thing between us was about. Sex. Really good sex. I didn't have time to think, not about anything. I put my hand over her mouth to mute her screams. She was fucking loud when she got excited, and as I tilted my head to the side, I caught a glimpse of *her*, like a shimmering golden light. She was leaning against the hood of a car, legs crossed, looking sexy as fuck. She looked right at me. I tried to look away but I couldn't and then she did it, she uncrossed her legs lying back, she lifted her gold dress right there in the parking lot. "Oh, fuck," I groaned pushing harder into Paula one last time. When I came down from my high, Sage was gone, and I knew I was losing my mind.

I want to slip into the world of dreams
because that is where I left you
In between the place of sleep and wake
Is where you'll be
I want to find you
And make sure you stay

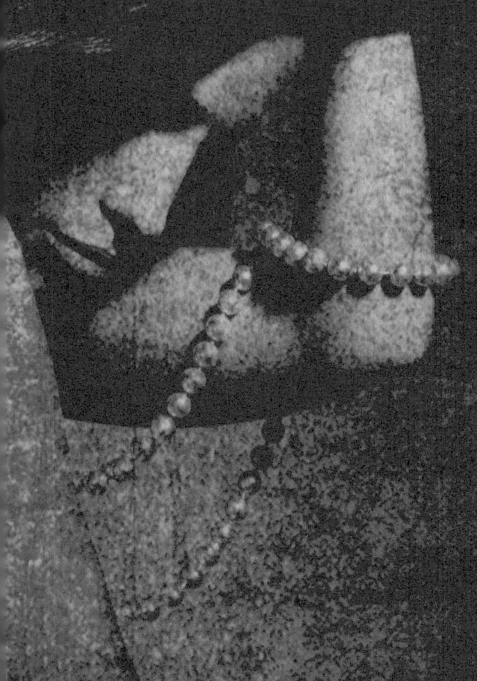

THIRTEEN
SAGE

Everything was dark, and the rain fell hard on the roof. The windows and doors felt like they were going to cave at any moment. The smell was worse when it rained, the carpets on the stone floor got wet, and it felt colder somehow. She comes in, and the little girl pretended to be asleep. The woman knew she wasn't because her eyelids fluttered.

"I'm sorry little one, sorry, so sorry." She didn't sound cruel or evil, she sounded afraid, and she sounds sorry. I heard the door open, and he came in. His boots are heavy on the floor.

"What do you think you're doing in here?"

"Just checking on the brat, making sure she's asleep." She stuttered.

He doesn't fall for that, he never does. He knows everything there is to know. From the slit in my eyes, I saw him grab a fistful of her hair. He dragged her away kicking and screaming. And the screaming didn't stop. The tears fell from the little girl's eyes, and she wished for once that when she got out of here, that she could take the ghost woman with her too. It wouldn't matter if she were a ghost out there.

I woke up in a cold sweat. Those dreams, they were the same every night, a story, the little girl's story. I dug out my notepad and started to jot down some notes. I had to talk to Siren about the dreams today. I had to know if they meant anything at all to her.

"Siren," I said over breakfast. She looked up from her espresso annoyed. I never disturbed her when she read. But I couldn't think about that now; I had to ask her. I needed to know if she knew anything.

"Yes," she answered.

"I-I've been having dreams, strange dreams that make no sense to me," I started.

"Dreams about?"

"A little girl, she's trapped in some kind of cabin, and she wants to get out. There's a man there and woman, and well monsters."

She laughed. "Monsters? You can't seriously be concerned about this Sage. It's just a dream."

"She looked like us, Siren and when I am in those dreams, I feel like those things are happening to me."

"It was just a dream Sage," she said dismissively, getting back to her paper. I should have known that talking to her would be no help. At least she didn't blow up about it. I wanted to believe her, that this was just a dream but why then did it plague me so much. I couldn't get the girls face off my mind. I could feel her terror, and it sent chills down my spine.

Sometimes when he thinks I'm not watching he stares at me in fascination. I have never been viewed at with anything but contempt, so it is something strange and unnerving. I tried not to read too much into it. I was not the kind of woman any man would be interested in, let alone Jake Cole. He is gorgeous and brilliant, a few of the many things I was not and will never be. Besides, I knew that he liked Paula from reception. I've seen them together at lunch or just strolling along the street hand in hand. That must be nice, being in love or in like, whatever it was. I was living in a dream yet again, letting myself get carried away by delusions. It was no wonder Siren thought I was a nutcase.

I'd finally started feeling more useful at the office, I dared not tell Siren this, but Steve and Jake started giving me more work. It kept me busy, made me feel like there was a purpose to all this. Nothing has changed at home, but thankfully Siren has had no reason to hurt me.

I'm deep in thought and don't notice when he comes up behind me.

"Hey, you wanna grab a bite to eat?"

I can't believe that he appeared just when I was thinking about him, well not about him, about his perfect love life amongst other things.

"I err, no," I managed. I can feel my face flushing. I placed a palm on my cheek to make sure he doesn't notice.

"No?" he asked.

"Yes." Why am I fumbling with my words? I felt like a blubbering idiot right about now, and that isn't a good look for me.

"So, it's a yes," he laughed, and I couldn't help but notice that he is an extremely good-looking man.

"No, it's a no," I gathered my papers and pushed past him. My face felt like it was on fire and I dared myself to glance back and couldn't believe that he was still watching me. With that thought, I made my way to lunch.

There was something about this place that wasn't like any other. For some reason, Siren didn't know about it, either that or she didn't care. I felt content here, at peace. It's a hippie joint complete with Rasta baristas and they made a mean strawberry tea. This has been my escape for the last few months. I was lucky to stumble upon it one day by chance, rushing to get out of the rain.

The smell of coffee lured me in despite the fact that I don't drink a drop of the poison. The staff was friendly, and this became my daily ritual. I had one thing that was just for me, and I intended to enjoy it. When you live a life of unease, even the smallest glimpse of gratification was like a soothing balm to the soul. This is what this small hole in the wall café was, medicine for my aching soul.

FOURTEEN

JAKE

I couldn't see Paula anymore. I couldn't fool around when all I wanted was Sage. She consumed my every thought. I knew how messed up that sounded. I didn't even know the woman well enough to be this intoxicated by her. But I was drawn to her, like a bee is to pollen like a moth is to a flame. We have barely spoken, but I just wanted to be near her. I wanted to know her. I didn't understand why I was so attracted to her, but I was. Everything about her pulled me in. She was intriguing and so incredibly smart. Paula just complicated things and I have never been one to lead a lady on when my interest was elsewhere. It has been an intense few months of fun, but that is all that it was.

Steve suggested that we give Sage a few novellas to edit and her work was incredible. She had an eye for detail and she never disappointed. The more I worked with her, the more I wanted to know her. She was a mystery I wanted to unravel. She hardly ever smiled, but there were times when she did exceptionally well on a story, and Steve commended her. She beamed, and I could feel it radiate throughout the room. I could listen to her talk about anything, all day. It was as if she were singing to me. I went home frustrated every single evening because I was so close to her and yet so damn far. It'd been months, and she wouldn't give me the time of day. She wouldn't let me near her. I'd decided that today was the day I would leave her no choice.

I knew she went out for lunch at the same time every day. I followed her once, well maybe more than once and I knew she sat at a small café nearby that no one knew about. She ate a whole-wheat sandwich and drank some pink tea. Her routine never changed, and today I wasn't just going to follow her around like a crazy man. I would sit down and make her talk to me or at least look at me. She couldn't avoid me if I were right in front of her. I got to the café, and my heart rate picked up. What the hell was wrong with me? I could do this. I had approached countless women in my time; she was no different. Was she? I waited for her to place her order and sat at her table twiddling my thumbs.

She pulled off her hood as she made her way over to the table and I knew she was surprised to see me sitting there. The effect this girl had on me was unnerving.

"Hi, Jake," she cautiously approached the table. I could see she was battling with herself on whether to keep walking. This spot seemed to be hers for some reason and I was sitting in it. I smiled inwardly at my genius.

"Hi, Sage, would you like to join me?" I asked looking into her beautiful eyes and deciding that there is no reason to beat around the bush. The way she looked at me excited me; I was at her mercy. I wanted to talk to her. I wanted to hear everything. Anything. I wanted her to tell me to get the hell out of her seat.

She seemed to consider it for a minute, but I didn't miss the fact that she surveyed the restaurant and the street before she hesitantly nodded and took a seat across from me.

I instantly got the scent of honeysuckle. We've been this close before, but we're surrounded by the stench of paper and old books but here I can smell it more acutely, and I am taken aback for a second. She shifts in her seat, obviously out of her comfort zone.

Her hair fell like a dark curtain around her lovely face, and I wondered why she would ever hide it. Her skin was perfect, the kind of skin that looked like silk and most likely felt like it. I thought about running my knuckles against her high cheek bones as she leaned into me.

"Thanks for joining me," I cleared my throat and grinned at her.

"Thanks for the invite," she said.

Her lunch arrived, and I figured that they pre-made her food by the quick service. I asked the waiter for an ice tea and a chicken salad sandwich.

She looked at me knowingly. "Did you follow me here?" she asked taking a sip of her tea which carried a scent as sweet as she was.

"Maybe," I admitted.

She looked out the window at the passersby and didn't respond. She wrapped her small hands around the cup, and I wondered what it would feel to hold them between my own. I knew I needed to get a grip.

"It's a nice place," I said motioning around us.

"It is," she smiled, and I had a feeling it had some special significance to her.

This place really was something. The walls were covered in artwork by local artists, and it gave the place a studio vibe. Every round table had a small vase with daisies in it. The waiting staff and baristas were all friendly and jazz music played softly in the background. There were motivational quotes in frames in between the paintings and there was a sixties hippie feeling in the air. The smells of fresh flowers and incense filled the air. I recognized the smell, something my mother used to light, Sage.

"So tell me about Sage?" I asked her.

"What would you like to know exactly?" she asked, taking a bite of her sandwich. I expected her to be nervous and unable to eat a bite, but I was pleasantly surprised that she wasn't.

"Well, I know the basics; it's in your employee file." I laughed.

"Stalker," teased, her mouth forming a perfect O.

I laughed. I liked this lighter, relaxed side of Sage. A side I had not seen in the time we've worked together. This wasn't the Sage I worked with every day, here, we're just a guy and a girl having a normal conversation, getting to know each other.

"What do you do when you're not at Sky Corp?" I asked.

"I read a lot and drink whiskey." She answered honestly.

"A whiskey girl?" I teased. "Who's your gentleman?"

"*Jack* will always have my heart," she giggled.

She's nothing like I imagined her to be. I expected to sit here in complete silence while she cowered into herself like she usually does. But this — I understand why I have been so enthralled with her.

She finished up her sandwich and tea, looking out onto the street. I sensed that she was somewhere else in her mind.

"What kind?" I asked letting my gaze rest on her cup.

"Strawberry," she answered.

I nodded, committing it to memory. We sat in a comfortable silence, me not wanting to disturb her peace.

"It was nice talking to you Sage Fenton, don't be a stranger," I added after a while. She smiled at me and even though I didn't want to leave the table or the world where Sage and I spoke to each other I knew we had to. There was something about Sage, something I wanted to unravel. Our lunch hour was over, and I got up first, leaving her to her thoughts and made my way back to the office with a grin I couldn't seem to wipe off my face.

FIFTEEN

SAGE

Talking to Jake was easier than I thought it would be. We started eating lunch together almost every day, and I slowly got better at it. I didn't feel as anxious as I once did. Siren didn't seem to know or care about what I did in the day as long as it didn't include talking to people about her and that was fine by me. I was starting to feel like a human being again, not an invalid.

I enjoyed the time we spent together. There were no expectations, just two people enjoying each other's company. A month ago, I'd gotten a hefty raise for all the extra work I'd been doing in the department. I opened another bank account and asked Steve to get HR to deposit my raise in there. He didn't ask questions. He never did. It was a nice chunk of money, and if I saved enough, I possibly could get a place of my own in a year or sooner.

"Where do you go to when you stare at those pictures," Jake considered me with interest one day over lunch. I hadn't even realized I was doing it.

"To a place long ago, Jake," I smiled. I don't know why I told him some things, but I did. I am comfortable with him. He had an easy way about him. "My parents died when I was very young, and it always reminds me of them, of the last place where we were all happy together. I look at the paintings of the ocean, and I can almost smell the sea air, and I can feel the sand in my toes, hear the crashing of waves."

"I'm sorry for your loss," he gently reached out to take my hand in his. I let him. I felt a surge of electricity coursing through me and I quickly drew my hand away.

"So am I," I say truthfully. "I guess life would have been a whole lot easier if they were still here with me."

"Do you have any other family?" he takes a sip of his Café Latte.

I want to say no; I don't want these conversations to center around Siren but no matter how much I despised her at times. I couldn't deny her existence. I just don't have to tell him everything.

"I have a sister. We're not close." I tell him, knowing that he won't ask more.

He nodded. "I know that feeling. I have a brother and sister, and we don't speak except if we're forced to attend a family function together," he clarified.

"Really?" I couldn't imagine anyone not wanting to have anything to do with Jake, let alone his siblings.

"I guess I'm a bit of the odd one out, Sage," he responded honestly.

"So am I," I smirked.

"Then that makes us a likely pair doesn't it?" He grins back at me, and I get that familiar feeling of out of control butterflies in my stomach that happens every time I am around him.

That night, Siren went out alone. She didn't ask me to go with her, so I turned in for an early night. I heard her getting ready and flirting on the phone with someone. I assumed it was another guy she intended to use and discard like trash. She used her beauty and her sex appeal to lure them in and then she pretended they didn't exist. I wanted no part in it, and as I lay my head on the pillow, sleep overtook me and my last thoughts were of Jake. I shouldn't like him as much as I do but I can't help myself. There is so much to like. Everything about him drew me in. It isn't just the fact that he was incredibly good looking, no, he saw me like most people didn't.

I woke up the next morning exhausted. My head and stomach ached. It felt like I'd been out drinking all night. As much as I wanted to call in sick, I didn't, and it wasn't because I was afraid of Siren this time. It was because I wanted to see Jake again and maybe talk to him some more. Our conversations, although light and short, were what I looked forward to the most every day. I finally felt like someone understood me. He was interested in me, in what I had to say. He didn't just see me as the quiet weird woman, but just a woman.

Jake and I were both extremely busy today, he had two manuscripts which were urgent and I was working on my first full length novel.

I walked into his office at the end of the day and he was sitting at his desk hunched over a manuscript.

As if he sensed my presence, he looked up, and his gaze held me in place. There was something about the way he looked at me that made me feel like mush inside. I took a deep breath, looking at my shoes to break the spell. This happened to me a long time ago, and that didn't turn out the way I'd hoped, I didn't want to go down this road again, not if it turned out the way it did. I didn't want to think about that now. I wanted to focus on work. I felt stronger than I had in a long time. I haven't had those disturbing dreams for days, and although my anxiety levels were sky high I didn't feel like my world was falling apart, and that was something to celebrate.

"I'm leaving, Jake," I stood in the doorway not wanting to get any closer to him than was absolutely necessary. The effect he had on me was that intense.

"See you tomorrow Sage, be careful out there." He grinned at me and I swore I stopped breathing for a few seconds.

I backed away, leaving him to his work. I patted my shoulder bag.

"And now to get this story in the right hands," I whispered under my breath. I looked over at the received post trolley and smiled.

Siren was not in the parking lot after work, she's always punctual, so I don't understand where she could be. I wanted to ask the guard if he'd seen her but I didn't want to draw too much attention to myself. This frustrated me, and I started pacing, running my cold hands together to try to keep them warm. Her car was parked in the usual spot, and I wished that I at least had the keys to sit inside and wait for her. I don't dare venture up to her office. That would be unthinkable. So I waited next to the elevator. It's freezing outside, and I hated the cold. It reminded me of things I don't want to be reminded of. My fingers ached, and I tucked them into my pockets. I heard the elevator door open, and I look up for Siren expectantly.

"Hey Sage," Jake greeted smiling at me like I am his favorite person in the world. "You're still here?"

"Just waiting for my lift," I responded kicking the toe of my Chuck Taylors on the cement. I wish he wouldn't look at me the way he did.

"I could drop you off at home if you'd like. You can call your driver from there. It's freezing," he offered. Why does he have to be so nice to me all the time? It makes it difficult not to like him.

"I wouldn't want to impose Jake. I'm sure my driver won't be much longer. She's probably just delayed with something important." I insisted.

I notice the relief flash on his face at my use of the words *she*. He was glad a guy wasn't picking me up. I smiled inwardly at that.

"Let me wait with you then," he said.

"It's really okay," I told him hoping that he would take a hint.

"It's no problem at all," he insisted.

I want to wait for Siren, but it's late and cold. I also

didn't want Siren to find us together. I make a choice. I would deal with the wrath later.

"Okay, I'd like to take you up on that lift," I knew I'd regret it, the minute the words left my mouth.

He looked like a child on Christmas morning. His eyes lit up and I couldn't help but smile. "Wait right here," he said.

I nodded. There wasn't anywhere I could go now was there?

A few minutes later he pulls up in a BMW HP4.

"What! I can't get on that," I exclaimed as he handed me a helmet and hopped off his bike to help me put it on.

"You're scared now Sage. I thought Whiskey girls were fearless." He laughed, and it's a dangerously good sound.

"I've just never been on one before," I whisper anxiously eyeing the beast.

It was truly a beautiful piece of metal in varying shades of blue and gray. I didn't know the specifics, but I'd seen this particular one in a magazine. It's supposedly deemed the hottest superbike yet.

"We're about to change that," he buckled my helmet, his gloved fingers brushing my neck causing me to shiver all over and I know it's not because of the cold.

He removed his brown leather jacket and insisted that I put it on. I almost drown in it, but the scent was enough to make any girl, even an inexperienced one like me swoon.

"Lucky me," I whispered with my heart in my mouth and my stomach did flip-flops a mile an hour.

He hopped on and tapped the seat behind him for me to do the same. He flashed me a grin, and I'm sold. I got behind him and leaned as far back as possible away from him.

"You've got to hold onto me Sage, not too tight though, just flow with me," he turned around and winked causing me butterflies, as he slipped on his helmet.

"Where are we headed Sage?" he asked.

I rattled off my address. It wasn't far from where we worked. We didn't give our company our real address; supposedly for safety reasons but I didn't see why I couldn't tell Jake the truth.

And before I knew it we were whizzing through the afternoon traffic; the cold wind made my nose scrunch up. It was not as scary as I thought it would be and I held onto him more comfortably liking the feel of him in my arms. I leaned onto his back and felt a contentment I had never felt before. I felt freedom.

This was better than anything I'd felt in a long time, and the tears streamed down my face and probably seeped into his t-shirt as I reminded myself that this was not something I could ever have or get used to. I was broken in ways he would never understand.

We pull up outside my apartment, and I hopped off reluctantly, already missing the feel of him. I desperately wanted to invite him in. The urge was so great, but the fear was even greater. She could be home, and there would be hell to pay. I started to remove his jacket, and he stopped me.

"Keep it for now," he offered me a heart-stopping

smile.

He hopped off and slowly unbuckled my helmet. He placed it in the storage compartment. When he turned back to meet my gaze, there were so many unspoken words which flowed between us.

The intensity of his stare caused me to look away. He removed a glove from one of his hands and lifted my chin to meet his eyes again. I could get lost in those eyes, lose myself, and lose my very soul. He brushed his cold knuckles against my cheeks so softly I swore it never happened and then he leaned in and did the unexpected. He brushed his lips against mine. He was so gentle; I shivered to my core.

"I always wanted to know what that would feel like, from the first moment I laid eyes on you, Whiskey girl," he whispered causing my heart to race inside my chest.

I released the breath I'd been holding and placed my hand against his chest.

There were suddenly no words needed.

He held me close to him and kissed the top of my head, reluctantly letting me go. Hopping back on his bike he winked at me before slipping on his helmet.

"Thanks, Jake," I managed to utter.

"Anytime beautiful." He took off, and I was left speechless. He can't mean that, nobody sees me that way. I don't see myself that way. I walked up to the empty apartment and showered and got into bed. I didn't feel like having dinner. I didn't feel like making dinner. I heard Siren come in after one am. She rattled around the kitchen and made her way to bed. I was grateful she didn't come in to disturb or harass me for not waiting up for her. She obviously had plans that didn't include me. I was sick to death of being at her beck and call, and soon I would get a driver's license and stop being dependent on her. I drifted back to sleep again. I was still able to feel Jake's lips on mine and smell his musky scent around me. I wrapped his jacket around me. I would have this night and tomorrow things would be back to normal. I didn't deserve someone like Jake Cole. He didn't deserve what Siren would do to him if she ever found out that I was falling for him, and I was. I was falling hard and fast, and there was nobody that could stop this, but me.

SIXTEEN

JAKE

I smiled at her this morning, and she didn't smile back. It was as if the night before didn't happen. I found my jacket hanging on my chair, and she was keeping herself exceptionally busy, so she didn't have to speak to me. I was taken aback. I thought she'd felt something, anything, even just the need to be friends, if nothing else. Sage Fenton was a complicated woman. Unfortunately for her, I'd decided she was worth the pursuit. I followed her to lunch again, and she let me join her at our table. She pretended I wasn't there and read a book, sipping her strawberry tea. I sat silently too, reading the morning newspaper. I walked her back and let her be. She wasn't in the parking lot when I left that night, and I wasn't surprised. I'd just have to try again tomorrow. I continued trying for two more weeks, but the monotony was getting to me. I needed to hear her voice again, not just the one that responded to instructions at the office or greeted me out of courtesy. I wanted to hear her giggle, maybe even laugh.

So I did the only thing I could do. I went full on Jake Cole. She went to lunch the next day, and I followed her like I usually did. We sat, and she ate and drank tea while reading and I watched her. When she got up to leave she couldn't get out of the door. It was locked, and she called for the barista and wait staff, and nobody came. She got frustrated and went to the back; even the staff entrance was locked. She stormed back out frustrated.

"Did you do this, Jake?" she shrieked.

"Yes," I answered simply not taking my eyes off the newspaper.

"Why?" she asked frustrated.

"You wouldn't speak to me," I offered.

"What, Jake, I talk to you all the time!" She declared exasperated.

"Not about anything that matters Sage," I retorted meeting her fiery gaze.

"What do you want to know exactly Jake," she growled.

"I want to know why you acted like the other night didn't happen," I got up to stand in front of her, towering over her.

Her gaze met mine, and she closed her eyes as she took a deep breath. I knew the moment I was getting through to her, when she shook her head, and a small smile played on her lips, I took that gap to wrap my arms around her and brought my lips down to meet hers.

"Jake," she whispered breaking away from me.

"This," she motioned between us. "This can't happen."

"Why the hell not? You're not married or seeing anyone." I respond irritated.

"How the fuck would you know that I'm not seeing

anyone," she said.

"I just do!"

"My life is complicated Jake."

"So is everyone's Sage but I'd like to get to know you. Just give me one date then, no more, and if you still feel that way after that. I'll give up. I'll let you be. Just give me that at least." I pleaded. I placed my forehead against hers.

She pondered about it for a few seconds, and she looked up at me.

"I can do that," she smiled. "But I cannot promise you anything more and you have to promise that you'll try to understand."

"I promise," I assured her, but I knew that this one date was all I needed to change her mind.

I unlocked the doors and let her leave. I watched her walk away, and I felt on top of the world. One date was all I needed. She would understand that I was seriously into her. I had never felt this way about anyone and I knew just what to do to show her.

Aflame

I am on Fire,

Pure,

I am consumed

I am trapped yet free

I am on Fire

Scorching

My feet refuse to touch the earth

I am on Fire

It is building within me

I am aflame

SEVENTEEN
SAGE

Siren never explained her absences over the last few weeks. She didn't say a word to me. She acted like I didn't exist and I wasn't complaining about that. I hadn't been on the receiving end of her temper in a long time. But a part of me was worried about her. She didn't look as vibrant as she always did and I wondered if she was ill. I couldn't resist asking her about it just because I was afraid of her reaction. She was my sister, and I had a right to know if she wasn't okay.

"Siren," I ventured over dinner one night with more conviction than I felt.

She looked up at me but didn't answer.

"Siren, are you alright?"

"Of course I am. Why would you ask me that?" she taunted.

"Well, you don't look so great," I hissed, under my breath.

"Says *you*," she laughed.

I rolled my eyes and got up to place my plate in the dishwasher.

"Did I say you could leave the table, Sage?" She asked.

"No, but I am done eating, and I want to leave the table now Siren." This was bullshit. I can't be treated like a fucking child anymore. Something's got to give.

She actually looked confused and out of her depth. There was something seriously wrong with Siren. Any other day I would be dead.

"I'm going out for the day tomorrow Siren," I said taking the gap given to me.

She looked up at me and didn't utter a word. I left the kitchen and had some whiskey before bed. That was a small victory, but I was not dumb enough to think I'd won the war.

Standing outside my building waiting for Jake, I can't believe that I agreed to a *date* and that I told Siren I was going out and that I actually am. She wasn't at home again, and I imagined her out sulking, getting her already perfect hair done and her manicured nails buffed. I decided to dress up today. I had on a long sleeved purple jersey dress, leggings and high heeled boots. My long hair was curled and over my shoulder in a ponytail. I wore a light multicolored beany and scarf. I never went on dates, so I hoped this was appropriate. He pulled up a few minutes later in a convertible. Who was this guy? Not that I am complaining, my attire wasn't exactly fit for a motorbike. It was a warm day even though a chill was in the air.

He got out and opened my door for me. A gentleman

too.

"You look lovely, as always Sage," he planted a kiss on my cheek which sent chills through me, in a good way.

'Thank you, Jake," I climbed into the car feeling on top of the world.

He asked me to trust him as he slipped a blindfold over my eyes. I wanted to panic, but I didn't. There was something comforting about being in his presence.

"This is weird," I confessed a few minutes into the drive.

"Just enjoy the anticipation," he teased.

We drove in a comfortable silence, music playing softly in the background and I must have dozed off along the way because I am awoken by a familiar scent, one I hadn't experienced in years but one I could never forget.

"You can take that blindfold off now," he coaxed. "Although I can think of a few things I could do to you with those on."

"What happened to no pressure," I laughed.

I took the blindfold off, and my eyes glazed over at the sight before me. The sandy shore stretched for miles, and the ocean expanded further than the eye could see. Our windows were rolled down as we drove down the mountain road. The view before me was breathtaking.

"Jake," I whispered, his name alone was a prayer of thankfulness to the universe.

"How did you know?" I whispered.

"You told me that this was the one place you felt closest to your parents and hadn't been to in a long time." He smirked.

"You listened," I couldn't stop the tears. This was the sweetest and most generous thing that anyone has ever done for me.

"Hey, this is supposed to be a happy moment Sage."

"It is," I responded, wiping a few stray tears from my cheeks. I was happy after a very long time.

"By the way, I always listen. There isn't anything more beautiful than the sound of your voice and the beauty in your thoughts."

We spent the day in the sand, talking and eating hot dogs. I hadn't eaten anything unhealthy in a long time, and I could imagine the eyebrow-raising Siren would give me if she knew. Jake was a perfect gentleman at all times. We walked hand in hand, and we collected shells of every color. I was content. I hadn't felt this kind of hope and joy in a long time. I remembered Molly and Dale and everyone that was taken away from me because of Siren and I swore that she would not take Jake away from me.

"You're more beautiful than beautiful Sage," he smiled at me as we lay on the sand, not caring if it got into our clothes and hair.

"That's not even possible," I laughed. "Not to mention, bloody corny."

"Is it now," he got up and leaned on an elbow.

I placed my hands on each side of his head, allowing my fingers to tangle in his hair and I brought his lips down to meet mine. It was the boldest and bravest thing that I have ever done, and I enjoyed every second of it.

"I think I'm falling for you Jake Cole," I whispered, looking into his eyes.

"Been there, done that," he affirmed as he placed his lips on mine. His kiss was gentle at first, but the pace slowly changed until I felt like I was swimming in a sea of powerful emotions. He kissed me like it's our last kiss. I let myself feel every stroke of his tongue and the intensity of my emotions. I allowed myself to taste the spiciness of his breath and the earthy scent of his cologne heightened my senses. I moaned into his lips, and it drove him to deepen the kiss even more. I felt every kiss deep within me. He didn't even realize the feelings he invoked in me. I was putty in his hands.

"We should go soon," I said, coming back to earth and breaking the kiss but lingering on his lips.

"But not right now," he whispered.

We lay there for a few more minutes, breathing each other in, the sand in our toes as our heart beats struggled to normalize. He rolled off me, and we lay side by side, looking up at the evening sky. We'd been here all day, but it felt insufficient.

I knew this day would have to end soon. But when it did end, I would carry its magic with me, and not even Siren could take that away from me. I turned to face him. He was even more handsome up close. His stubble grew out, and I reached out to touch it. It felt prickly on my fingers, and I reveled in the sensation.

"Can we do this again, some time," I asked hesitantly, afraid if this was a once off thing for him. He turned toward me and smiled. His eyes locked on mine.

"I would love to do this every single day, but I'll settle for this being a weekend thing." He grinned. I nodded and looked back up at the sky.

When he dropped me outside my building that evening, I leaned in and kissed him on his full lips. I felt braver than I have ever felt in my life.

"Thank you, Jake, for an amazing day," I leaned my head against the headrest.

"…of many to come, I hope?" He questioned almost shyly.

He kissed me again and unbuckled his seatbelt to get out. He practically hopped over his hood to open my door. What a showoff. I smiled because I liked it. I got out and planted a kiss on his stubble cheek.

"Good night, Jake Cole," I whispered.

"Good night, Whiskey girl."

EIGHTEEN

SIREN

I felt her slipping away from me every day, and I didn't know how to keep a handle on things anymore. She thought that I hated her, that I wanted to control and punish her. How far from the truth that was. I agreed that my methods were sometimes very ruthless but how else was I going to make sure that she listened. Sage was stubborn, she always had been, and she needed to understand that I was protecting her from what the world could do to her. She wasn't strong enough to face it yet, on her own. She needed me to guide her and make sure that no one harmed her. She wasn't experienced in the ways of the world, not the way I was, and it was my duty to teach her.

The world hung people like Sage out to dry. They drenched every ounce of life, heart, and soul from them and discarded them like a carcass in the desert. The only reason Sage has survived at all was because of me. And yet she was becoming more and more ungrateful and selfish. How dare she go out today? Did she not know that these things require my consent? I looked at myself in the mirror, I should go out too, but I didn't feel like it. When have I ever not felt like going out? She's got me all miserable and depressed reminding me of her sorry self. It was that man, her boss. I saw them together earlier. She'd let someone in, gave him our address. She stood there like a blushing teenager when he picked her up. I would have to do something about it. The only way Sage learned was the hard way. It has always been that way since we were children.

I wandered into her darkened room and turned the light on. The room was dull and dreary and had no character, just like Sage. It expressed nothing about the person living in here for several hours of the day. At least she was tidy. I have noticed changes in her recently, and it unsettled me. We were fine, living an uneventful life before that boss guy came into her life. And yet, she insisted that they were just friends. I wanted to believe her because I didn't seem to have the energy for her stupidity anymore but I felt like there was so much that she's been hiding from me.

"What are you hiding from me, Sage?" I said to the empty room while scouring her shelves of hundreds of books. The bookcase towered over me, and I didn't understand her fascination with books. I realized that there wasn't anything in here after ruffling through her drawers and pulling out a few books. It was just plain, boring Sage in here. I didn't know what I expected.

I should have some wine, relax and wait for her to return.

A few hours later, she arrived, right on time as I knew she would. She greeted me and started on dinner. She didn't share anything about her day, but she looked different. Lighter somehow. I wanted to ask her about it, but I chose not to.

I should be freaking out. I wanted to bash her head against the tiles and watch as blood dripped down her fucking head. It took everything in me not to. I'd let her delude herself into thinking that she hasn't done anything wrong. But her actions have threatened our way of life, and I was ready to do something about it. I had a plan. I smirked to myself. I was right. Hurting her now wouldn't achieve anything. No! I'd wait it out.

NINETEEN

JAKE

Sage was nothing like I'd imagined her to be, no, she was far better. I have liked women in the past, but she was different. She made me want to settle down. I knew that was thinking ahead, but I've heard that if you meet someone and you get that feeling of home with them, you shouldn't let them go. It's what I felt like when I was with her. I didn't have to pretend to be anyone else. I could just be Jake. Just Jake. It's been two weeks since our date at the beach and we have slipped back into our lunch routine. But I wanted more of her, more time with her, not just an hour of her mind, but hours of it. I wanted to listen to her speaking, telling me about the hundreds of books she'd read. Most of which I have read too. Sage was beautiful in a way most women would envy. I'd been surrounded by beauty my whole life but no-one compared to Sage Fenton. She was truly something special.

"Where are you today?" she asked, snapping two elegant fingers in my face. I hadn't even noticed her looking at me. We'd been sharing a comfortable silence, her reading, a latest *Paulo Coelho novel, The Spy*, and me staring at my tablet, at reviews on a publishing forum.

"Just thinking about how I'd like to take you on

another date," I grinned.

"Oh, you had to do that didn't you?"

"Do what?" I feigned shock, placing my hands over my mouth.

"The panty-dropping grin," she laughed motioning to my lips.

"I have one of those? I didn't notice. It hasn't seemed to have worked on you."

She threw her head back and laughed so hard I couldn't help but join in.

"So, has it worked? Are you ready to drop them?" I took her hand in mine across the table, rubbing circles on her knuckles. She stopped laughing and instantly flushed. "I'm kidding Whiskey girl, but I'd like to have that second date you promised me."

"Did I promise you one?" she smiled.

"I believe you did."

"Then I better make good on that promise," she laced her fingers through mine. It was a simple act but so much more than I could have expected a few months ago.

Have you ever just been so connected to someone, so much so that the emotions you felt was inexplicable. That was how I felt with this woman.

"Sage, I've really enjoyed getting to know you better," I said as we got up to leave. I drew her close to me. "I've really enjoyed these lips on mine too," I traced my thumb on her bottom lip. Her breath hitched, and her eyes never left mine. They dilated when she was close to me. My mother always told me that, it was an indication of deep affection for someone. The more dilated the eye was, the more you loved a person.

"I-I've liked that too," she whispered, leaning in closer to me.

"Which part Sage, you've got to be more specific."

"This," She got up on her tiptoes and placed a chaste kiss on my lips.

"Nah, you don't get off that easy." I picked her up and held her to my chest. She giggled. She actually giggled, and it was the sexiest sound. And I kissed her lips more fiercely. I knew in that second that I so much more than liked kissing Sage. I so much more than liked everything about her.

The beachside restaurant was stunning, and I was instantly pleased with my choice. The place had rustic décor and was light and airy. It was late afternoon so the patio we were sitting on, which as a few feet away from the shore, was dimly lit. Each table had a lantern on it to cast that extra bit of light needed for a pleasant dining experience. They specialized in authentic seafood, but there were other options available for those wanting something different. I looked at Sage sitting across me. Her hair was loose and fell wildly around her shoulders. I could see flecks of sand in it, and I want to rub my hands through it to dust it out, only to feel her close to me. The woman before me in a white cotton dress, her skin bronzed because of a full day in the sun, her eyes ablaze, and her cheeks sun-kissed captivated me in a way no other woman before her ever could. I hung on her every word, watched her every move. I noticed the way she stared out at the ocean, lost in thought.

She had a story, and I wanted to hear the whole of it, not just the parts that sounded pretty, but everything. She reminded me a lot of my mother sometimes. They were opposites in looks, but before we had the whole fall out, she had the same kind of fascination with the world, the way Sage did. She also took on more than she could handle and settled for less than she deserved. There are moments when I looked at Sage, and she had this terrified expression on her face. I wanted to ask her about it, but I was afraid that if I did, it would break the magic. So I let her be and hoped that when the time came, she'd open up to me.

The waiter arrived, and I asked Sage if she had any wine preferences. She smiled and shook her head.

"Go ahead and order, I would love anything you do."

I ordered a bottle of Sauvignon Blanc which I knew went perfectly with seafood. The waiter returned, and I asked him to leave the bottle as I would like to pour my lady a glass. Sage flushed again.

"I like that look on you," I whispered when the waiter left us.

"What look is that?" she asked.

"Oh, just the bashful Sage look, it's kind of cute,"

"Did you just call me cute?"

"My exact words were, it looks cute on you Sage, and you can hardly be called cute. Sexy. Breathtaking. Those are more up your alley."

"Flattery will get you everywhere Jake," she beamed and took a sip of her wine.

"Mmm, "she moaned, "This is delicious."

Those sounds from her lips were not meant for a public place. It completely distracted me, and I found my eyes drawn to her lips.

"So any recommendations on the menu since you've been here before? I don't go out much, and my diet is pretty bland, so I will go with whatever you suggest." I wondered how a woman like Sage wouldn't go out much. I wanted to ask her about it, but I knew it would be crossing that unspoken line.

"The line fish and calamari never disappoint," I offered.

"Then that is what I will have," she beamed at me, and I loved the innocence in those simple words. I was not the kind of man that would control a woman. I can't speak for the bedroom, but in day to day life I like a woman with independence. But I liked the trust she placed in me, in this simple gesture. When the waiter returned, I placed our orders and refilled our glasses.

The wine seemed to have relaxed her even more, and she constantly reached for my hand rubbing circles on it. Her touch was driving me insane, and I wanted to focus on things other than what she was causing down south.

"Are you distracted Jacob," she asked, batting those pretty eyelashes at me.

"Why would you say that?" I asked her, genuinely interested. Can she read my thoughts? It was then that I realized that her small foot was on my crotch under the table.

"You're going to make me lose my shit, woman," I hissed.

I gently pried her foot away and placed it down. I shook my head, and suddenly I was the one flushing. That was one sexy as fuck thing she did, but I can't think with my dick right now.

"You're different tonight, Whiskey girl," I observed when our meals arrived.

"Different how?" she asked in between chews. "Gosh, this is amazing," referring to the food.

"Freer," I said holding her gaze. Time seemed to stand still when I looked into her eyes. I knew how cliché that sounded but it felt like that.

She pondered this for a second and smiled. "I think I am freer Jake. For a long time, I have been caught up in a limbo, I haven't been living my life the way I should, but you've taken me out of my comfort zone, so yes, in a way I am freer, unrestricted and happier than I have ever been in my entire existence."

I wondered why she would have held herself back from living as much as she obviously had. What makes a woman as beautiful and bright as Sage, live in the shadows? She doesn't belong in the shadows, not when she exuded that much light. It was as if she'd forgotten how to live. I knew by saying what she had, she had just let me into a part of her world but there was so much more I wanted to know. I needed to know everything about Sage. I had to know all of it. But I would let her be the judge of when she should let me in.

I took her hand in mine and brought it to my lips. Her eyes were instantly ablaze. I let my lips linger.

"Take me home, Jacob Cole."

And she didn't have to explain what she meant.

TWENTY
SAGE

I couldn't believe I was here, in Jake's apartment. It's late, he turned on a few lights, and the glow in the room was ethereal. His home reflected him. It's not overly masculine. There are rows and rows of books perfectly shelved in bookcases in almost every room. There is an electric fireplace in the living room which was sparsely decorated in earthy tones of brown, green and beige. His stainless-steel kitchen and dining room were one open space, and the same earthy tones carried through. This home had heart and soul. The home of a reader and writer.

The view of the city was spectacular at night, and I stood in front of the floor to ceiling windows and marveled at the beauty before me. A thousand stars, fallen from the heavens were at my feet. I felt like I could step out and get lost in them. Jake came up behind me and wrapped his arms around me. He placed a kiss on the crook of my neck and had me leaning into him, extending my neck further to grant him better access. He placed his hands on my hips, as he firmly held me in place. I felt steady and sure and yet I was floating on a cloud. I didn't want to come back down to earth, not tonight. I wanted to live in this world, where it was just Jake and me, in this beautiful apartment with the stars and the scent of a day at the beach surrounding us.

"I want to shower, Jake," I whispered leaning into his chest. "Get some of this sand out."

"Okay," he placed a kiss on my neck.

I turned to face him and leaned up on my toes and kissed his neck. He responded by scooping me up in his arms and carrying me to the bathroom.

It's large and masculine. Everything was stainless steel and gray marble. This was no doubt his sanctuary, and I could barely breathe at the thought of the time he spent in here.

There's a double shower on one end and a corner bathtub on the other end. I could see us enjoying these together. I immediately blushed at the thought that this was *my* idea. Whatever happened to me? This was your time Sage, I reminded myself. This was what you wanted, and he obliged. Don't be a coward. Be brave.

I slipped my dress off slowly, never taking my eyes off him. I stood in just my bra and underwear. He stared at me almost nervously, and I smirked.

"I thought a big boy like you would have had some experience," I said seriously, reaching back to snap off my bra, then dropping it to the floor. I slid my panties down and stepped out of them slowly. I'd never felt as bold as I did at that moment.

He literally gaped as I entered the shower and turned on the facet.

"Your turn Jacob Cole and make it entertaining," I

teased as the warm water cascades down my body. He undressed and walked towards me. He was more glorious than I imagined. His body is lean and strong, not overly muscular but I could tell that he kept fit. I felt the urge to touch every inch of him. He stepped into the shower and held me close to him.

"You know you don't have to do this now. We can wait Sage."

"I want to live Jake, I want to live tonight, and I want you to make me feel alive."

I place my hand over his heart. "I need you. I want you. This. This is what I want."

The water fell over his long hair and down his beard. I cupped his face and laced my fingers through his stubble. His eyes closed as he touched his lips to mine. I wanted to see every expression. I wanted to remember every moment. A whirlwind of emotions circles us. His hands burned against my flesh, and I knew that I would forever be branded by him. He touched every inch of me with reverence. His kisses intensified, and they scorched their way into my soul. The feel of his lips against my skin sent tremors to my very core.

"Be alive Sage," he hissed, before lifting me against the cold shower tiles and burying himself in me in one fluid motion. I gasped at the coldness of the tiles and the warmness of him inside me. We moved together in a symphony, no lyrics were needed. I held onto him as if my life depended on it. The waves of arousal thrashed against us. And when we let go, I felt my world spinning off kilter. It was like nothing I'd experienced before, and

I knew that I wanted more of this, more of him, more of more. I knew that my world would never be the same without Jacob Cole. He was that missing piece of the puzzle of my life.

The one thing I never knew I needed but could never live without.

TWENTY-ONE
SIREN

She was exceptionally late. It's past three am. She should have been home a long time ago. I wanted to call Steve Hart, but he'd think I was losing my shit. I don't know what I was thinking, fucking that loser. I guess when you're just starting out in life; you take what you can get. And I took. It was the only way to keep an eye on Sage. Unfortunately, he'd started getting too fond of Sage. He pitied her, wanting to help her, even save her, from *me*. There was no other explanation why he wouldn't tell me about her secret love affair with the handsome Editorial Assistant.

Sage was thirty-two years old, and she could technically do whatever she wanted except she was not in charge here. I was. She should have let me know that she was not going to be home on time. I was slowly losing a handle on this situation. This kind of shit didn't happen to me. I should never have given her that kind of freedom. I thought that if I did, I would be able to manage this situation which seemed to be spiraling out of control. That she wouldn't fight back. I heard the front door at just past three thirty am. I wanted to leave it until later in the morning, but I have never been one who lets sleeping dogs lie. I got up and met her in the hallway, just as she was creeping into her bedroom like a common thief. I switched the light on, and she looked startled.

"You freaked me out, Siren," she gasped, her hands on her chest.

She looks disheveled. Just fucked hair, her clothing a royal mess and was that a glow? I think it was. For the first time in a long time, Sage looked fucking happy.

"Where were you all day?"

"Not now Siren, we'll talk about this in the morning," she sighed loudly, her chest heaving. I couldn't help but feel that she was annoyed at me for questioning her.

"No, we will talk about this *now* Sage," I hissed.

"*You* talk about it. *I*, on the other hand, am going to bed." She defiantly reached for her door handle.

What was happening to her? Why am I not able to keep her in check anymore? Maybe she needed another lesson? Maybe that is what she wanted all along. The hand incident wasn't enough, was it?

I walked toward her, and she turned around quickly placing her hand on my chest.

"You don't want to do this Siren," she warned. Her eyes met mine, but she didn't shy away as she usually did.

Was that a fucking threat? I was in charge here, not her and I would have to teach her that. I grabbed her hand, knowing it was the injured one and probably still hurt and twisted it so hard she screamed. Her screams echoed through the apartment causing a shiver to course through me. Her screams always fueled me, so I twisted her hand further, all the way around her back and shoved her against the wall. She struggled to get free of me and tried to back kick me. I hit her on the back of her head with my own head, and the force made me feel slightly dizzy. That gave her the gap she needed to run into the living room, heading for the door.

"Where will you run Sage? To him? How will he protect you from me when you can't even protect yourself?"

She flinched and immediately picked up a vase, a very expensive collector's piece and threw it at me. It crashed inches next to my head, and I was closing the gap between us in seconds. I lurched for her and gripped her flimsy dress at the front. She lost her footing and fell to the ground arms and legs flailing. She continued to fight me to no avail. I had to give it to her; she's shown some genuine courage this time. But it will never help her. There was no way that poor Sage could get the upper hand on me and it was about fucking time she realized that. I straddled her and punched her head hard, hard enough that the wind leaves her.

She's knocked out cold, but I knew it would not be for long. I had to act fast to subdue her. I rushed to my room and grabbed scarves from my drawer. I walked back and almost expected her to be struggling to get away, but she was still out. I flipped her over and bound her hands and legs.

I dragged her sorry ass to the bathroom. Thankfully she wasn't heavy. I dragged her up to the edge of the bathtub and threw her in. She bumped her head, but I didn't care. I started filling the bathtub with ice-cold water. She came to and immediately started struggling on her restraints. Thankfully I'd done a good job of it.

"You ungrateful bitch, after everything I have done for you," I spat.

"Please Siren, we can work this out." She pleaded.

I pushed her into the cold water, and she howled in agony. I laughed, and it echoed off the four walls.

"Siren!" she shouted as she came up for air. I closed the tap and sat on the toilet lid, her hair in my hands.

I pushed her head under the water one more time and watched as her eyes grow large and her cheeks puffed as she tried to desperately suck in some air.

I brought her up for a second and continued this torture until I thought she's had enough.

"I could kill you Sage, and nobody would give a fuck." I taunted. "Nobody would look for you or care that you're gone. Not Steve. Not that loser you're fucking. Nobody. I could kill you, and that would be it, do you realize that?"

She choked and spluttered. I let the water out in case she tried to drown herself, but I left her tied up and freezing in the bathtub overnight. There was no escaping the wrath of Siren. She'd crossed the line, and she would have to learn this time.

It was about fucking time.

TWENTY-TWO

JAKE

I hadn't heard from her all of yesterday and today. It wasn't like her to skip work and not tell anyone. She didn't own a cell phone, so I couldn't reach her. Who doesn't own a cell phone in this day and age? I'd spoken to Steve about it. He promised to try to contact her. I knew that was bullshit because she didn't have a cell phone. I didn't understand how he could be so flippant about it. Was I wrong about the fact that he cared for her?

By midday, I was worried sick. I couldn't just sit around here doing nothing. The woman I have come to care about deeply is missing, and I would be damned if I sat around fucking hopelessly. I grabbed my keys and left the office heading straight for her apartment building. It was expensive inside, tasteful. I asked the doorman if they'd seen Sage, only to be met by a guarded no. She told me she lived on the second floor, apartment number ten. I took the stairs up one at a time, and knocked on the door a few times and there was no reply. I started pacing the hallway. I knocked again and not expecting anything; I turned the doorknob to find it unlocked.

That's strange. "Sage!" I shouted entering her home. The living room was a mess, a broken vase on the floor, carpets and pillows were scattered everywhere, obviously out of place. It looked like there was a struggle in here. I hoped that she hadn't experienced a break in, but that didn't explain the open door which had not been tampered with. I felt panicked now, the sweat starting to coat my neck and palms. I walked around the rest of the small apartment which was thankfully in a better state. I couldn't help but marvel at the tasteful décor and paintings. Truthfully, nothing in here reflected Sage. I imagined a more relaxed home, soft edges, nothing like this – rigid. I walked down the passage, and there was what looked like a study to the left, I couldn't be sure as it was a darkened room. I stepped in and turned on a light; there were a daybed, bookshelf, and desk. I assumed that her bedroom might be straight ahead. I entered the main bathroom first, which was opposite the study, and the place was a soaking mess like a pipe had burst, either that Sage had left the tap open to flood the place. None of this made any sense.

"Sage?" I shouted entering the room down the hallway without knocking. It's empty. Her room was immaculate and didn't look like anyone had slept there. Everything was undisturbed.

I decided that the mess in the apartment may be reason enough to call the cops. While I waited I knocked on the neighbor's door to find out if they'd heard any disturbance last night. An old woman opens the door but left the catcher on.

"Yes, can I help you?" she asked warily, not making eye contact. She was old, at least seventy years old, her wrinkles covered her eyes, and her gray hair hung loosely around her slight shoulders.

"Yes, Ma'am, I wanted to know if you know the lady that lives across here, Sage Fenton. There has been a disturbance at her place, and she's been missing for a day or two. I- I'm, Jake Cole, her boss." I slipped a card from my wallet and handed it to her through the small space hoping that it would ease her tension.

She frowned and looked down at the card and then at me. Her blue-gray eyes were piercing through me.

"No, I don't know anything about that woman, and I would prefer it if you didn't bother me." She slammed the door in my face and I stood in the hallway feeling more confused than ever. How can a neighbor behave that way? I just told her that Sage was missing. Was she not worried, if not for Sage, but for herself? If a burglary has happened, another one was likely to follow. I walked back to the apartment but decided to stand out in the hallway not wanting to disturb anything in case this was a crime scene. I was going out of my mind. This connection I felt to her, was nothing like I'd ever felt with anyone before her and I wasn't about to let her slip through my fingers like that.

"Where are you, Sage?" It took everything for me not to break down in that hallway and fucking cry.

TWENTY-THREE

SAGE

I opened my eyes slowly, and I was in the backseat of Siren's car. The cream leather stuck to my cheeks. The motion made me sick to my stomach. My head hurts. My body ached all over. I recalled the night before, and I was afraid for what was to come. My legs and hands were still bound, but I managed to struggle into a sitting position. I looked outside, and I didn't know where we are headed. We're definitely out of the city now. I could see the landscape stretching for miles all around us. This part of the world was mountainous, I don't know how long we've been driving, but it had to be a while because mountains like these were miles away from the city. She looked straight ahead as she drove. I knew she was aware that I was now awake, but she didn't acknowledge me.

"Where are you taking me, Siren?" I asked. The more I struggled against the restraints, the more it hurts. She looked at me from the rearview mirror, frowning. I know how she hated being questioned, but I can't help it. I needed to know.

"You decide that Sage," she stated calmly.

"What the fuck is that supposed to mean?" I spat the words, angry, helpless and utterly hopeless.

"I am beyond angry. You've disappointed me, and there is no going back. But let's start with this. How are things with Jake, Sage? She taunted.

"He is my boss Siren, he's a friend," I said close to tears. I can't say much more; I have to convince her that, which is all Jake, is to me, a friend.

"I am not the one you should be afraid of Sagie," she mocked and I have to bite my tongue from saying something stupid, something that will land me in a ditch somewhere. I hate that berating nickname.

"I think it's time you learn a few things Sage, things I have protected you from for so long, things you're forcing me to rehash. I didn't want to do that to you Sage, but you've left me no choice. She glances out of the window. "It is time. You have done everything in your power to destroy the life we have. You fight against me every chance you get, and it is about time you understand the repercussions."

"Where are we going Siren?" I asked her again, more calmly. I had to play along. Suddenly I want to survive this, I want to get the fuck away from her, and I want to live.

"A few crucial stops until we reach our destination." I looked at myself in the rearview mirror, and I looked disheveled and unstable. Just the way she wanted me to look.

"And what is our destination, exactly?" My voice had that quivering edge to it, and it made me angry that I couldn't be brave and fearless.

"The truth."

She stopped the car, and I felt relieved. I needed to use the bathroom desperately. I hated being at her mercy. But I didn't say anything. I just let her drag me out and untie my ankles. They felt numb, and I had to let the blood flow back to my legs. The pins and needles felt like they would never end, the ice, the heat, the agony. I wanted to scream, and writ as the blood flow returns, but I didn't. I just remained on the ground not wanting to move.

I looked up at the sky. The sun was high, so it was past midday. I imagined that I was an animal carcass dying on the ground, just waiting to the vultures to come and feed on me. Anything was better than the torture I have endured my whole life. I got up into a sitting position.

"Where are we?" I finally asked looking around me. My throat felt dry suddenly, and I could only croak out the words. The road looks vaguely familiar, and I sensed that I'd been here before. We were parked on the side of the road closest to a rocky rise. Across the road, I saw a barrier, and I could only imagine how steep that drop was. There was a road sign that warned against slippery roads and rock slides.

"Are we here so you can finish me off?" I asked her.

"No Sage, on the contrary, I am here for other reasons," she jeered as if I am as stupid as anything. She laughed at me, and grabbed my arms roughly dragging me to my feet and across the road. She was so much stronger than me and because my hands were tied, I didn't even have a chance.

"What is this place?" I asked her when we got to the

other side.

"You'll see Sage," She laughed. I don't understand what was so funny. But this kind of cryptic shit is just like Siren.

"Do you remember the day Molly Kramer got hurt?" she stared out over the rocky canyon in thought.

"You mean the day *you* hurt Molly?" I corrected her. She turned and frowned at me.

"Sage you can point fingers all you like, but this isn't the time for it. There is something I need to show you," she held my gaze, and as much as I wanted to say no, I did as she said. I nodded. She proceeded to take my hand in hers, and I felt an overwhelming urge to vomit.

"Concentrate Sage," she demanded through gritted teeth, and I could do nothing but obey. I felt like I was falling like I was sinking into an abyss. I tried to scream, but the words didn't come out. Finally, I came to a stop, and I could safely open my eyes. But I'm not at the gorge anymore; instead, I am home, on the street where we lived with our grandparents. Everything looked outdated, like I'd slipped back in time for a moment. I looked around, and Siren wasn't with me. And then I saw her…

I could see myself walking to school with Molly, her red hair in two ponytails, bouncing along behind her. It was a contrast to my black hair which is in a single ponytail. Molly looked sure, confident, while I walked with my shoulders bent. I noticed that she kept looking across the road to the left at the short hedges. She covered her mouth to stifle a giggle. The strange thing was that we were not even talking. I edged closer to the two little girls. I wondered if they could see me although I doubt it. This was just a dream. When I looked closer into the hedges, I saw two other children hiding in there. I recognized them from school; it was Ben Harris and Lucy Carlisle. Why hadn't I noticed them there before? Molly and I came to a stop at an old hedge.

"You seem really sad today Sage," she smiled.

"I'm okay Molly; I'm just tired I guess." I started to wring my hands on my long sleeve t-shirt.

"Is it because of your parents? She asked. She seems genuinely concerned.

I thought about her question, and I nodded. "I do miss them," I said softly pulling my ponytail over my shoulder to braid it. It was a nervous habit I had.

"What's that?" she motioned to my arm, my long sleeve t-shirt had ridden up a little, and the cuts were evident.

"If I tell you, do you promise not to tell anyone?" I leaned in and whispered.

"Of course, we're best friends," she nodded.

I glanced over to the bush, and I knew the other two kids are within earshot. Don't say anything Sage. But she can't hear me.

"My sister, Siren, she bullies me a lot," I said quietly.

"Your sister?" she looked at me questioningly.

"She hurts me, all the time; she bullies me and treats me badly. She's the one who did this to me." I looked at the ground, tears starting to form. "It seems to give her some kind of satisfaction to do that," I sobbed. "She does it where my grandparents can't see," I rid up my skirt and my sleeves a little more to show her the bruises.

Molly looks horrified.

"You're insane Sage, you know that?" she spat, disgusted.

"Molly, you've been to my house, you've met her, and you know how cruel she can be," I say.

"You're crazy Sage Fenton, a crazy weird girl!" she shouted at me and spas and scoffed.

"How dare you, Molly?" I growled. It hurt that she would say that to me. I just opened up my heart to her and told her something that nobody else knew and she mocked my suffering. I was angry.

I pushed Molly so hard she fell off the sidewalk onto the street. She scraped her elbow and knee, the flesh raw and bloodied. She tried to get back up, but I kicked her, really hard in the stomach. I pulled Molly by the hair and dragged her back onto the pavement.

"You do not speak of this to anyone Molly Kramer, or I'll throw you in front of a bus." I hissed.

"I promise Sage, I won't tell anyone" she cried, tears streaming down her face now dirty.

She stumbled up and looked at me in desperation… no that was fear. She was scared of me.

I felt cold all over. I was petrified, unable to speak or breathe.

"What have you done Siren?" I whispered.

"I've done nothing Sage that was all you." She laughed.

I gasped. "What the fuck?" I backed away from her. She let go of my hand, her childish sinister laughter still echoing in my ears.

"That doesn't make sense. What the fuck are you doing to me?" I asked launching toward her only having her sidestep me. I kicked my toe on a rock and fell to the ground. "It's not how I remember it at all." I sobbed, not caring how pathetic I sounded. I felt helpless. What kind of sick mind games was she playing with me.

"No Sage. That is how you chose to remember it," she said. "You, my dear, have a selective memory. You need to know everything Sage, but you're not strong enough, and you can't do it alone. You need help," she shot. Her irritation was evident.

"And I bet you're going to help me, Siren?"

"You'll see," she taunted.

I wanted to slap her so hard maybe even push her in front of the next vehicle that came pass here or even over this fucking godforsaken cliff, but she's my sister. I cannot do that. I won't do that. None of this made any sense.

"You know this place, Sage," she looked at me and motioned to the cliff below us.

I do know this place.

"But – how?" I gasp.

"I need you to concentrate again Sage." She said. And I closed my eyes, and did as I was told. The displacement wasn't as bad as it was before. I opened my eyes and I was sitting in a car next to -. I'm started because it's me again, just a younger version of me.

I sat in the backseat playing with my dolls. They're beautiful dolls my father bought me for Christmas. I named them, Sage and Siren and they're arguing again. Mom and Dad are upfront, and they're smiling at each other. I could see that her hand rested on his thigh as it always did on a long drive and her pretty curls bounced when he whispered something funny under his breath, an inside joke just meant for them. She turned around and smiled at me. I smiled back. "I love you," she mouthed. I could barely see her in the dark, but I knew what she was saying, she always said that. I concentrated on my dolls. The road was really dark, and I kept looking outside. I hated the dark. I pulled my dolls closer to me.

"Don't be afraid," I whispered.

"It can't get in here sweetheart," Dad said.

"I know Daddy," I smiled. I trusted everything he told me.

"The darkness can't get in if I surround myself with light." I chanted those words over and over again under my breath.

I saw the light in front of us and leaned forward to see, but I dropped my dolls.

"I dropped my dolls, Mommy," I sulked.

She unbuckled her seatbelt as she usually did when I did something like that and leaned to the back. She couldn't reach them, so she stretched a little further.

"Got it," she smiled.

"Daddy," I said excitedly, "The light. See!" He turned to glance back at me.

We go towards the light really fast, and everyone is shouting. Mom, Dad, Me, even my dolls. The car was moving around a lot, and we move around with it. I heard seatbelts snapping, and suddenly there's blood everywhere. So much that I can't see anything before me. I dropped my dolls from my hands.

I wanted to shout.

Mom!

Dad!

Sage!

Siren!

But the words don't leave my mouth. I can't breathe. My head and chest hurt.

The darkness was getting in Daddy, it's getting in.

It got in and swallowed us whole.

"What the hell was that Siren?" I yelled her. I was covered in sweat. My heart was beating rapidly, and I was finding it hard to breathe. We hadn't jumped. I just thought we did. I thought I was dying. What else would explain what I have just experienced?

"It was a memory, Sage."

"Whose memory is it?" I pleaded.

"It's yours," she stated.

I don't have a response to that. We get in the car silently. There are no restraints this time. I don't need them. I will go with her. I can't describe what I have just seen but I know she can, so I will go with her and hope that when all this is over, some of it will make sense.

TWENTY-FOUR

JAKE

A week, it's been a week since I'd seen her. The police said there was no sign of forced entry so there isn't much that they could do. "She's probably just a messy person, Mr. Cole." The slightly balding officer told me. "People have a right to up and go whenever they like. The porter informed us that although she left in a hurry, there was nothing suspicious about it. She drove out of the building, the footage was clear. There was absolutely nothing odd here." That all sounded perfect except I knew Sage, I spent more time with her than they had. I liked to think that I knew her better than most people did. And for one thing, Sage did not drive so it was nearly impossible that she would have driven out of that building. She lived alone; she'd told me so herself. I just wished I had more information on her sister, estranged or not, I had a feeling she would help me.

"Steve," I knocked once and entered his office. He motioned for me to take a seat and I did.

"I have to know that she's okay," I shrugged.

"Where will you start Cole?" he asked me.

"I have no idea but I have to try."

He nodded. "I hope you know what you're doing

Cole."

"It's been a week, and I cannot simply sit around waiting for her to come back. I know it may not make sense to you but trust me, I have this feeling that something isn't right with her," I looked down at my pants and proceeded to dust some non-existent lint off. I wanted to do anything but look into his face. I didn't want to be angry with him, but I was. Steve didn't seem to be fazed, and I wondered whether he knew something that I didn't.

"I understand Cole; take all the time you need."

I wanted to shout at him and tell him to just be clear with me. He knew her for far longer than I had and I could not doubt that I'd seen the way he looked at her, he cared about her, although he would never admit it. I got up to leave but before I closed the door behind me he stopped me and reaching into his desk drawer he pulled out a small piece of paper.

"You are going to need this," he said. I looked at it and he'd scribbled an address on it.

"It's her grandparents address." He said simply. I breathed a sigh of relief. I needed this information. This was my first lead.

I got into the elevator, and I had no idea what I was going to say to her grandparents when I got there, but that was where I was headed. They were my consolation prize but in the absence of information on her sister in her employee file. I had no choice. I also noticed that she gave an incorrect address on her job application. I had to make sense of why she just up and left especially when we were just getting started. Maybe, getting some insight into the person Sage really was will help me figure out where she could be.

The day after I went to her house, I took a drive to the beach. I hoped she'd checked in somewhere. That she needed to clear her head. But she was at none of the hotels on the strip we frequented lately. Had I done something to hurt her? Did I move too fast? Sage meant too much to me to simply pretend that everything was okay. I thought she felt it too, the connection. I am not the kind of guy who goes off the rails like this, especially not for a woman, but Sage, she's different. I had no idea if she will ever be back, or where she was, but maybe her grandparents would be able to give me some answers. Every second she's away from me, the harder it got to breathe, the harder it was to exist. She's the best thing in my world.

My phone rang, and I looked at the screen and frowned. And just like I usually did, I let it ring and go to voicemail. I have more important things to do.

"I'll find you, Sage," I said as I got into my car and let the road lead me to the truth I was so desperately searching for.

TWENTY-FIVE

SAGE

Siren came to yet another stop, and I knew this one. I'd been here several times when I was younger, but I hadn't visited it since we moved out to the city. I used to come here every weekend when we lived with our grandparents. I would sit on my parent's granite tombstone and talk to them. Tell them about my day and the latest trouble Siren was getting us both into. I wished that they could talk back to me, just once, to give me the answers I was so desperately looking for, but they never did. They failed me. They'd abandoned me, and now I didn't even know what Siren's plans were. I knew she was hateful and dangerous, but would she kill me? She was so unpredictable when she was angry.

I hadn't even had a proper shot at a real life. I thought of Jake, his beautiful face, the way he looked at me every time we were together. For the first time in my life, I felt like I had something to look forward to. I thought about our time together which seemed like a distant memory now. Did all of that actually happen? Did he really feel the way I thought he did? He didn't see me the way everyone else did, he never pitied me, and he never saw me as Siren's shadow. I prayed that I would never have to introduce the two of them.

He saw me, the real me, there were no pretenses between us. I was just Sage. But I wondered if he'd have felt the same way about me if he'd met her first, would he have liked her more? Would she be more suited for him than me? I can't think like that. It is just the kind of thing she would say to me, as she chipped away at my confidence bit by bit until there was absolutely nothing left to lose.

We got out and made our way to the place our parents rested.

"Take my hand Sage," she said, reaching and grabbing hold of mine as I reluctantly obliged.

"Close your eyes and see."

"I don't understand what you mean, Siren," I have seen this more times than I can count. When she glared at me, I did as I was told.

"Open them," she commanded.

I do, and nothing has changed, everything is the way it has always been.

"Read Sage," she demanded, and I obey.

In ever loving memory of Lester and Mary-Ann Fenton
Loving parents of Sage Fenton
Always loving, always loved.
"It always read Sage and Siren!
Always!" I cried in horror.

"Did you change it, Siren? You can't be that cruel," I howled.

"I didn't change it, Sage. It's always been this way."

"What the fuck do you mean Siren?" I asked her distraught. "Did they forget your name? I saw it, I read it, I traced those words with my fingers for years," I said backing away from her.

I fell into the dirt and I knew I was probably on someone's grave, but I didn't care.

"You're doing this to punish me, to taunt me for disobeying you."

"You're not that special Sage," she sat down next to me and picked some wildflowers. "You can't be that dumb."

I wanted to lash out at her and ask her what she meant. I hated her so much for what she'd done to me and for what she continued to do. She'd always been a heartless bitch, but today I understood that she was so much more than that. Siren Fenton was pure unadulterated evil. She thrived on the hurt and pain of others, and she reveled in. I looked at her now so content, observing me as if I am not even worthy to be beside her. She knew exactly what she was doing; she was trying to drive me back there. She was trying to make them put me away, the way they did the last time. Only this time, it would be for good. I couldn't let her do that to me. I couldn't go back there. Not now and not ever.

TWENTY-SIX

SAGE

THIRTEEN YEARS AGO

I didn't want to be sent away, but after the initial incident, another one occurred. I'd found out that Dale had a new girlfriend and to say that I was sad about it, wasn't adequate. It was heartbreaking. I felt the pain in the very fiber of my being. I couldn't breathe. I couldn't sleep. I couldn't live or exist in a world where Dale wasn't mine. I wanted to close myself away from the world, but Siren wouldn't let me. She told me that it was time to move the fuck along. There was no use crying over the past and what could have been.

"Men are a complication Sage, just like friends, just like anything that distracts you from your purpose in life," she'd sneered. I wondered what the purpose of my life was because it didn't seem like I had one.

It wasn't me who'd hurt him and yet I was the one who took the blame the way I'd always done. Siren told me that he deserved what he'd gotten. I hated what she was implying, and the way that thought embedded itself into my mind, making me feel like those were my thoughts too. She had no reason to hurt Dale, but she did, all because she was jealous that there was someone else in my life that might see me for more than she made me believe I was.

His new girlfriend lived in our apartment building. Stacey Jones. She was pretty with blue black hair and black eyes that sparkled. She had the body of a goddess, and I felt like a child in front of her. I hated how short I was and how I never seemed to gain an ounce of weight. She was a first-year medical student, intelligent, beautiful, perfect, all the things that I wasn't. I would look at her and wonder whether Dale ever thought of me anymore. Had all thoughts of me been wiped away so quickly and easily? They'd met at the hospital while he was recovering from his injuries and I always questioned if he'd told her who I was and whether she was revolted by me when she passed me in the hallways.

I wanted to ask him about it, and one day I decided that I would. There was no restraining order against me, and I decided that before there was one, I would get my chance to tell him I was sorry and beg for his forgiveness. I didn't want it to end like this. We may not be together, but I didn't want his last thoughts of me to be of Siren beating the hell out of him. Maybe I would tell him about Siren too, and maybe he would understand. He was always considerate. I waited until Siren was out when I did it. I sneaked over to Dale's apartment which was just a few blocks away. It was raining heavily that night. I tucked my coat around me and made a run for it. Dale lived on the ground floor. I wanted to go to the front door and knock, but I hesitated. I didn't know why I was so afraid. I shouldn't be afraid. I decided to go around back and peek in through the living room window, make sure he didn't have any guests, and that's when I saw them together. Dale and Stacey, his hands were all over her the way it used to be all over me. She was moaning into his neck the way I used to. He was holding her and kissing her the way he used to hold and kiss me. They were lost in each other, lost in ecstasy and I was an onlooker. I turned and ran, the tears streaming down my face. It was too much to take in. It really was over between us.

When I got home, I soaked in a hot bath for a long time, allowing the water to soothe my tired muscles. Siren came home, and I heard her shuffling around. The next day the restraining order arrived. I was to stay away from Dale and Stacey and a warning that I should appear at the Glenleaves Institute in the morning for a thorough psychiatric evaluation or I would risk the charges being returned. I knew Siren had something to do with it and I didn't have the energy to fight her anymore. She had all this power over me, and I had given it to her. I would never be free. I never went for the evaluation. I'd all but given up struggling against my fate, but Siren did, and before I knew it I was apprehended, medicated and harassed for the next five years. There were things I had to endure in those walls that I cannot think about. There were things that I saw within those walls that have etched their way into my consciousness and kept me up at night. My sister did that. She's found yet another way to twist and manipulate me. She was a sadist, and I hated her.

TWENTY-SEVEN

SIREN

We arrived at Grace's house, and I immediately felt the familiar nausea building in the pit of my stomach. The smell of the small town itself was sickening, old and worn, dirty and pathetic, but as my grandmother opened the front door and the stench of old fabric reached my nose, I almost hurled right there and then. She looked surprised to see us, her brown eyes wide with shock and was that a hint of horror? As usual, she didn't acknowledge me, just Sage. She didn't see anyone but Sage. It had always been that way. With Sage being the center of attention, I took a seat on the swing seat to watch this happy reunion play out.

"Sage," Grace said hesitantly. I noticed that she wiped her old grimy hands on her apron anxiously and I wondered if she'd even washed them.

"Gran," Sage said lovingly.

What the fuck was wrong with her?

"Please come in," Grace moved aside and gestured for Sage to enter.

"Siren," Sage looked over at me.

I saw the old woman's eyes widen, she sighed and gently shook her head. I smiled inwardly. I loved making her uncomfortable.

"Oh yes, do come in Siren," she offered sarcastically.

Despite my reluctance, I got up and entered the familiar shithole. Everything was still the same, from the old carpets to the ancient furniture. Family photos hung on the walls. In them everyone smiled and pretended that life was one fucking daydream.

Grace shut the door and showed us into the living room. I sat next to Sage on the old brown couch. The anxious quivers of her hands were getting to me. I placed a hand on hers to still her. She looked at me warily, and I pitied her. How was it possible that one person could be this weak and vulnerable?

"I'll be right back," Grace said. "I just want to put some tea on," she wobbled away, her old ass wobbling along with her.

"Why can't you be nice to her Siren?" Sage asked.

"Because I don't fucking want to Sage,' I hissed.

"Why are we here anyway?" she asked me confused. I wondered whether I should just let her suffer a little more but decided she's going to suffer anyway.

"Just ask her about the accident," I leered.

She looked at me dumb and confused. Why does Sage always have to be so pathetic?

She nodded and settled into her seat looking around longingly like she's lost in some happy memory of a time long ago. Sage has always been this way, and it was what made me dislike her. She tried to see the good in people, in situations, and things. Except for me, she never saw the good in me. She never saw what I did for her, or how much I'd sacrificed to make sure she lived a normal life. She never thanked me for saving her from *this*. I can imagine Sage working in some diner as a waitress or worse as a saleswoman. I watched her as she rubbed her hands together nervously. She's always edgy, always mousy. What did that Jake guy see in her anyway? I sighed.

The old woman entered after what seemed like a fucking eternity with a pot of tea and two cups. The bitch forgot about me. It's been so fucking long anyway.

Sage looked at the tray.

"I'll go get another cup," she stammered nervously.

She got up to made her way to the kitchen. Grace sat down awkwardly. She didn't look at me. I didn't expect her to.

Sage returned, and there was a knock on the door. She set the cup down and offered to get it. Grace declined and told Sage to take a seat and pour herself a cup of tea. All this formality was a farce. I knew the demons that lurked in these very closets.

As Sage poured a third cup, Grace entered with a young woman about our age. Her telltale red hair and glasses told me this was Molly Kramer. She wore a diner uniform, a frilled apron, and tennis shoes.

I watched in amusement as Molly took a seat across from Sage.

"Hi Molly," Sage said sweetly.

"Hi Sage, I – I didn't know you were back in town," Molly said.

Grace looked anxiously from Sage to Molly and offered to get another cup of the tea.

"We just got here actually," Sage responded too cheerfully casting a side glance at me. I say nothing. It was interesting how things played out sometimes. I watched the shift in Molly's gaze as she looked at the doorway praying for Grace to return. I grinned. I loved this part.

Grace returned and nervously finished up pouring the tea into cups.

She handed one to Molly, then Sage. She picked up one and asked Sage to hand it to me.

Sage obliged and handed it to me. I reached out to take it, and just when it was within my reach, I let it fall to the ground.

"I'm so sorry," Sage said meeting my gaze.

"It's alright Sage, go get a rag and forget it," I glared.

"Can I get you another cup?" she asked apologetically.

"No, I hate tea anyway," I answered her coolly.

She disappeared, and I watched Grace and Molly exchange a glance I am used to. They say nothing. They're afraid. I can sense it.

Sage came back and took her seat next to me.

"It's good to see you again, Molly," she smiled and I almost vomited at the old adoration in her voice. She never thought herself any better than these losers in this town. She always saw herself as the underdog, and that was why she was treated the way she was. Sage was never popular in school. In fact, she was a fucking outcast on two legs. It was a wonder that she even graduated. Those loser kids saw her as the plague. Nobody dared associate themselves with her unless it was to humiliate her. She was Sage Psycho Fenton.

"Molly has been stopping by often and checking up on me," Grace proudly smiled sat Molly as if the sun shone out of that huge ass of hers.

That fucking old bitch never spoke of us that way. I wanted to get up and slap her until she begged me to stop but I didn't.

It wasn't my moment.

After Molly left, I watched as Sage and Grace tried to awkwardly communicate.

Sage tried to include me in their conversation to no avail. Grace's focus was on Sage, as it should be.

"Tell me about the accident Gran," Sage said softly.

I watched Grace carefully as she sighed and decided what to say. For a second I thought that she may say nothing. Her pale skin looks paler, almost translucent. The weight of the burdens she'd carried seemed to weigh heavily on her.

"I only know what you know Sage, what I have told you growing up. It happened out on the ridge, at night, you were on your way back from a week-long holiday at the beach. The three of you -," she stopped and started sobbing.

Grace always played the victim and played that role exceptionally well.

"Four – you mean four Gran?" Sage said.

"No Sage, I mean three, just you, your Mom and Dad," Grace said sobbing. I looked at her, and I wondered how much it took for her to say nothing, all these years.

"And Siren?" Sage asked, looking to me for affirmation.

"Sage," Grace said sympathetically.

I watched as Sage got up horrified, looking to me for help.

"Gran, where was she when the accident happened?" Sage shouted in disbelief.

"Sage, I have no idea," Grace whispered.

TWENTY-EIGHT

JAKE

I'm outside an old colonial style house. The garden was overgrown, and the shutters needed painting. I don't know why I noticed these things, but I do. This was where Sage grew up. I wondered what she was like as a young girl, growing up in this small house, playing games in this small garden before me. I got out of my car and paused. I wanted to walk right up to the door, but then I noticed it, a blue Mercedes, the one that's often parked at the office when I got in and gone when I leave. It's hard not to miss. It's top of the range.

I remembered Sage loitering around it sometimes. I figured this was the person who gave her a lift sometimes. I wondered who this person was to her. I suddenly had the urge to wait a little longer. I needed to think about this. Why would Sage leave me without a fucking word? What if I've been right all along and she was married or some shit like that. What if me being here caused her more trouble? She'd told me that she traveled with a woman, but I knew that people lied sometimes.

I got into my car and jotted down the registration number of the Mercedes; maybe it'll come in handy sometime. I drove into town and decided to grab a bite to eat at a local diner. I don't know why I wanted to wait, but I had a gut feeling that I should. I needed to know where my lady was and I would not leave until I do.

"Can I get you anything honey?" a woman about my age asked. Her hair was red, and she wore thick-rimmed glasses.

"Just some coffee thanks," I continued to stare out of the window. This street was small and quaint the diner fitted in perfectly. I could not help but think about those movies, all kinds of shit seemed to happen in small towns like this one. My mind wandered back to Sage. Was she with that Mercedes owner right now? Was she okay? All these questions plagued me, and I realized that I didn't have an appetite after all. I pulled out my cell phone and started reading random posts on Facebook to bide time, technology finally coming as a useful distraction.

"Here you go," the waitress placed the coffee in front of me. It smelled awful, I expected a fresh cup, but this looks like it's been standing for a week.

"You're not from around here are you?" she leaned her hip against the table.

"No, actually," I answered as politely as I could. I have never been one for small talk. It annoyed the shit out of me.

"You here visiting someone then?"

"Just trying to locate a friend." She's nauseatingly forward, and I answered her only to try and end the probing.

"Well, I know a lot of people around here, and I might be able to help." I glanced up at her, and she looked at me like I was a fucking cheeseburger.

"I seriously doubt that." I'd hoped that my brashness would deter her, but she seemed to be a sucker for awkward situations.

"Look, thank you, but I think I'll be fine on my own." I got up and pulled my wallet out. I slipped out a bill and the picture I've been carrying of Sage slipped out. She immediately bent to pick it up, giving me a show of her cleavage

She looked at the picture, chewing her gum and then she froze. "Is this Sage Fenton?"

I snatched the picture from her. "It is. Now if you'll excuse me." She might know Sage but there was nothing that this nosey woman could say to interest me. She seemed like the gossip monger, and I didn't need that right now. She nodded. I'm surprised that she didn't say anything further to me but rushed off to the next table. Her behavior seems odd to me, but I didn't want her poking around in my business.

I left the diner and stood out on the curb. I did not miss her staring at me through the window. I gave her a wave and started walking. I needed to clear my head before I gathered up the guts to face Sage's family.

TWENTY-NINE

SAGE

I looked to my sister for affirmation, but she doesn't say a thing. She just sits there cross-legged. She lit up her electronic cigarette and grinned at me slyly.

"What do you mean Gran, how can you not know? Siren why won't you say something? Why are you sitting there so fucking silently?"

"Sage," my grandmother addressed me softly. I have heard that tone before, and I have just about had it with people treating me like a fool. This has been the order of the day my entire life. Protect Sage from herself. Protect Sage from her madness. She walked over to the glass cabinet, and I knew she was going to bring out the old family albums. My grandmother handed me the albums that are familiar to me. I spent countless days sobbing over these very pages growing up, wishing that my parents would come back to me. Their smiles beaming back at me were such a comfort then. It was a cruel reality to wake up in a world where they didn't exist. I push them back.

"I don't need to see these. I have seen them a thousand times. I want to know what you mean about Siren." I hated the look of pity in the old woman's eyes.

"Look at them Sage," Siren hissed. "And really see

them."

I sighed and reluctantly opened the first one knowing that on the front page was a familiar picture. I have seen it so many times that it was etched into my memory. It was one of the earliest pictures of Siren and me in a glass hospital cot bed. But that was not the picture staring back at me now. There was only one baby and under it, the name Sage Fenton. I paged through the rest of the album and slammed it shut. This was a sick mistake.

"I can't do this. I don't understand any of it. I've got to go!" I shouted at them both. "I don't know what kind of game this is, but it's fucking messed up, and I want no part of it."

"Sage!" my grandmother shouted, but I was already in the foyer. I could hear Siren's mocking laugh behind me. Despite my reluctance and my grandmother being clear that she didn't want me in her home anymore, I returned when my grandfather died. I came because she was family and I wanted to be there for her. I came even though I was not welcome in this house. I paid for the fucking funeral. I took care of everything even with the fallout. So now, I cannot understand the lengths that Siren has gone to, to make me look and feel like I am losing my fucking mind and the fact that my grandmother seemed to be playing along. Was this her ultimate punishment? Making me feel like my world wasn't what I thought it was? She was sicker than I ever imagined.

I rushed out of the door and started walking down the street briskly until I broke into a run, my Chucks hit the ground below me and my heart pounded in my chest.

There was only one place I needed to be right now. I ran until my chest hurts. I climbed through the rundown fence and walked through the weeds which were still as long as I remembered. I disappeared into them almost completely. I started climbing the ladder up to the old water tower, my safe haven, the one place where I'd always been able to clear my head and focus. When I got to the top, I took a moment to take the old town in. It had never been much more than that to me, yet another old town. It was never truly my home. Not without my parents. I had Siren, but over the years I knew that I was not as important to her as she was to me. So I learned to survive alone. This was the place I came to when life got too hard to bear, the one place I felt the most like me.

"Still running away Sage," she said derisively, and I couldn't help but roll my eyes. She followed me. I cannot believe the nerve she had. She sat down next to me, close enough that we were touching. This was the closest I had been to her, and I couldn't for the life of me believe that this woman was not only my sister but my twin. Surely we should be connected in some way, if we were, I never felt it. All I have ever experienced is her wrath. When we were younger, I thought that we would grow up close. Stick together. It was us against the world. We would trick guys together by going to each other's dates, that kind of thing. But life has a way of never happening the way you plan. I am appalled by her closeness and shift away, but space is limited up here.

She laughed when I did. "That's really mature, Sage."

"Siren, can I just have this, a few moments to myself?" I asked taking a deep breath and closing my eyes. I should have known that she would never let me be alone. All I wanted was to collect my thoughts.

"You should be thanking me, Sage, not being a little bitch." She hissed under her breath.

"I don't know what the fuck you're doing to me or what you're trying to achieve by all these mind games, but I am not falling for any of it, not anymore. When are you going to get tired of making my life a living hell?" I don't want to cry, I don't want to feel helpless, but I do.

"Siren, what is it that you want from me? You've taken everything I held near and dear, and you've destroyed it."

"There are things Sage which you fail to see, things you should see, things that will help you understand that you and I are no different."

I sneered at her. She was so full of it. Everything she'd shown me so far was a lie. They were carefully concocted lies. Ways to trap me further in her web.

"I am nothing like you Siren, nothing!"

"How can you be so sure, sister?"

"I just am, I spent my whole fucking life allowing you to treat me in the worst possible way and I am tired, I don't deserve this. I don't."

"You'll never be free Sage, not as long as you believe you're the victim."

"I hate you, I hate you so much, and I wish that you never existed." I stood up and lurched toward her, and for once, she looked afraid.

I grabbed hold of her arm, and she struggled to

break free,"

"You wouldn't hurt me, Sage. You don't have it in you."

"If you do, I do too." I glared at her, and she shuddered. But as much as I wanted to make her suffer she's right. I am not like her.

"Sage!" I heard his voice, and I thought I was dreaming, I looked down and there he was. I wanted to hit her, I wanted to throw her off this fucking tower, but his voice was all I could focus on.

"Jake," I whispered. What is he doing here?

"Go to him Sage, let him help you, you're going to need it," she said.

"You don't get to say that to me, Siren. You're the reason things are the way they are. I can't go to him. I don't deserve him. I'm so broken. No one needs that in their lives. I was wrong to let him think that there was a chance for us. There just isn't." I released her and slid down, my back against the tower, sobbing.

She scowled at me. I should have known she wouldn't care. She doesn't have a compassionate bone in her body. I can't believe I let her in. For a second when she told me to go to him, I thought she was actually looking out for me for once.

"You really are pathetic," she stated.

She's probably right, but it doesn't give her the right to say it.

"No Siren, you are, you are pathetic because you're lonely and fucking messed up. I won't stand for this anymore. You do not get to dictate to this part of my life.

Not now and not ever."

I know I was treading on dangerous ground but after all I'd been through, I did not care. Not now. She destroyed everything good in my life, and I was not about to let her destroy the best. I looked down at Jake, and I knew what I had to do.

"Remember that everything from here on out happened because you left me no choice." She looked at me in that cruel and sinister way.

"We'll see about that Siren," I hissed.

THIRTY

JAKE

She made her way down the water tower slowly, and relief flooded me. She ran into my arms, and I held her close. I kissed her hair and smelt her familiar honeysuckle scent, and I couldn't help it when tears that formed in my eyes.

"I thought I'd lost you," I whispered into her neck. "Why didn't you tell me where you were, Sage, why?"

"Take me home Jake," she sobbed, and I held her close to me.

"I will baby," I said scooping her up in my arms, feeling the rightness of this moment in that simple act.

I don't know why I made my way here of all places. I left the diner earlier, and I decided that I needed some time to think, I needed some time to breath and the water tower seemed like the perfect place to do that.

When I saw a pair of slender legs hanging off the ledge and those familiar Chuck Taylors, her hair was blowing in the wind; I wanted to fly to her. To take her in my arms and soar away, away from this place and everything that has ever hurt her. I have so many unanswered questions, but all I want to do now is give her what she's asked for.

"I need to tell you so many things Jake," she

whispered.

"You will, but not right now," I said holding her and leading her to my car.

The drive was longer than we anticipated and she was asleep for most of it. She was restless and kept talking in her sleep. We stopped for a restroom break, and I called Steve to let him know that I'd located Sage and that we were on our way home. I asked for a day or two, and he agreed. She didn't have an appetite, but I knew she had to eat, so I ordered her a bagel and some water. We sat in silence, each of us in our own world. Mine consisted of silent prayers of thanks that she was here with me. I don't know what I would have done if I'd lost her. There was no doubt that the battles she was fighting were too much for her to bear. I just hoped she knew that I was not going anywhere.

When we finally got into the city, we stopped at her apartment for her to pick up a few things. She didn't want to be alone, and I wasn't ready to let her out of my sight either, so it made sense for her to live with me. That was the one place I knew she would be safe. I felt an overwhelming urge to protect her. I don't know half of the things that she had been through. But I knew that she would open up to me when she was ready and when the time was right. She was distant as she gathered her things, walking around in a daze. I could understand that this place held painful memories. I knew she was suffering and I wished that I could take it all away. I gathered her in my arms and held her close.

"You're not alone Sage," I assured her, kissing the top of her head.

She held me closer and kissed my throat. I led her out of the apartment, and she didn't look back. She needed to be away from this place, and I was glad that I was the one she'd turned to.

Later that night, I woke up to the touch of her fingertips trailing my body. I noticed that she'd switched the night light on and she was already undressed, her leg thrown over mine. Every part of me felt electrified. Her touches were that intense. I let her feel every inch of me, trailing her way down my chest, to my stomach and finally into my boxer briefs. She stroked the length of me, and I closed my eyes and allowed her to take the lead. I didn't say a word. But then, when the sensation of her hands working me became too unbearable, I flipped her, so she was straddling me. I looked into her eyes which were now tourmaline orbs with flecks of honey. They were ablaze, with lust, or was there more behind them. I trailed my hand lightly over the skin of her breasts, her stomach and I held onto her hips. We didn't speak but gave in to the burning need to be connected. She slid onto me, and we connected in every sense of the word. I felt flames engulf my body. I felt her burn into my mind, my body and my soul, my Sage. The woman I wanted to fight for and save. She was my greatest quest and my greatest need. Her movements were calculated, she was in charge, she owned me, heart and soul, and when she moaned my name, throwing her head back, her hands holding onto my thighs as she clenched around me, I gave in, I let go, losing myself in her. For a second, I lost all reason. This woman did this to me, she alone, would be the death of me.

When we came down from our high, she climbed off me, and I cradled her in my arms. She fell asleep instantly. I brushed a few stray strands from her face. She was so beautiful. There was such content on her face as she snuggled up to my side. I can't have her close enough. I wrapped my arms around her, and as I dozed off, her dark and hungry gaze was the last thing I saw.

THIRTY-ONE

SAGE

I woke up to the sound of the shower. Jake was up already, and I had to resist the urge to climb in there with him. I looked around at his bedroom which was different shades of blue and gray. *Our* bedroom, I thought to myself smiling. It wasn't official, but things sure seemed to be moving fast with us. My body seemed to have a mind of its own as I made my way into the bathroom. I'm already undressed for the occasion and find myself stepping in behind him as he's shampooing his hair. I wrap my arms around his torso, and he isn't startled. Instead, he turned and pulled me closer to him, placing a kiss on my forehead. He proceeded to pour some of my shower gel into his hands, warming it under the spray and lathering my body, lingering over my breasts and taut nipples. We don't say a word because none are necessary. I just let him explore me as he makes his torturous way down to my core. I looked into his eyes which are ablaze with need, and I let out a moan as he slipped a finger into me. I clenched around him, throwing my head onto his shoulders. I held onto his strong back as his finger works its magic.

"I need you," I hissed. "All of you. Now."

He turned me around and bent me over, and before I could beg again, he'd filled me. His movements were slow at first but picked up pace quickly.

"You're amazing, babe," he whispered. He held onto my shoulders, dropping to my hips, and I felt completely filled. "I can't – are you close – "he could barely get the words out, and I felt myself clench around him as we both let go. He turned me around and kissed me hard, out of breath. I felt giddy with satisfaction. We washed each other off, and I exited the bathroom first after brushing my teeth.

I walked over to the wardrobe where my clothes now hung, and for the first time I didn't feel the need to wear skinny jeans and a hoodie. I don't feel nervous or afraid anymore. I don't want to hide. This was a new feeling, one that I could get used to. I slipped into a blue and white striped pencil skirt, a white shirt and blue heels. My hair fell all the way down my back. I saw Jake gulp as he exited the bathroom making his way over to where I stood.

"I take it you like," I said slyly.

He nodded and wrapped his arms around my waist, kissing my neck. Would I ever get bored of these feelings he invoked in me? Every touch seemed to set me ablaze. I leaned into him, feeling the hardness of his chest against me. The scent of him was surrounding me. I was safe, and I was free. I didn't have all the answers. But I had what I needed right here.

"You, Whiskey Girl, are going to make me late and get me fired," he laughed.

I giggle and stepped away from him.

"I'm making breakfast," I tell him, making my way to his kitchen, letting him get changed undistracted.

I walked into the stuffy office space, and for once I am glad to be here. I am slightly overdressed but still glad to be here.

"In my office in ten," Steve barked when he walked past my desk.

I forgot about the fact that I would need to answer for my absence.

I get my notepad and walked into his small office.

"You should open some windows in here Steve," I tell him cocking an eyebrow at him.

He considered me and laughed, shaking his head.

I don't laugh back. I don't know what could be so funny.

"Just work Sage, meet your deadlines and I don't want any trouble," he said firmly.

"Understood boss," I got up to leave, saluting him

"Oh and Sage, don't mess up Cole, he's the best I have," he said.

"I thought that I was the best you had, Steve," I smirked, winked at him and shut the door behind me.

What the fuck did I just say to Steve? That was not called for. And why was he not surprised.

Jake is engrossed in a manuscript and I decided that I should pick us up some lunch from the staff restaurant.

I was waiting in line when that bitch Paula decided it was necessary to bump into me.

"Sorry weirdo," she looked back at me over her shoulders.

Besides the fact that she was acting absolutely immature, I was so sick of people thinking that it was alright to treat me that way. What the fuck is her deal anyway? And then it hit me, she'd probably seen Jake and I together and figured we were now an item. He'd ended things with her long before we even got together. It was about time I taught that bitch a lesson.

I picked up our food and asked for some beetroot salad on the side.

She was sitting at a table with another receptionist, Lacy. I stopped by their table and paused, smiling at Paula who looked at me like a parasite. I leaned in, looked her in the eye and proceeded to dump the whole bowl of beetroot salad on the front of her starched white shirt.

"You fucking – "she started. She shuffled up and tried to wipe off the beetroot which just made it worse. Her face had turned the color of her shirt, and I laughed out loud. She glared at me readying herself to throw a myriad of insults my way.

"Nah ah ah," I cautioned, placing a finger to her lips. I bent down and whispered in her ear.

"We wouldn't want to talk about you and Henderson in finance now? Do we? I bet there are a lot of people who don't want that to get out,"

She looked at me horrified.

"That's a good girl," I hissed straitening up and turning to leave. "Always so submissive, aren't you?" I shouted over my shoulder.

Why didn't I do that sooner? The bitch was horrible to me from the moment I started working here.

I thought about Siren and where she was right now. Would she be proud of me for standing up for myself or would she judge me? I didn't care. This was my time, Sage Fenton's time. I was tired of living in her shadow, answering to her and everyone else. I was about to get everything I deserved and more, starting with my fucking freedom.

THIRTY-TWO

JAKE

I looked at her and I could not believe that she was mine. I'd spent so much time trying to win her over and then when she disappeared, I imagined that all sorts of awful things had happened to her, and now she was within my reach. She's different somehow, more confident and secure. She's not afraid all the time or looking over her shoulder. I felt like the visit to her family gave her the answers she was looking for. I still liked to believe that I was some of the reason for the change in her but I knew that she fought some unspoken battles that even I wouldn't be able to comprehend. I didn't push her about it anymore. I'd tried getting her to open up to me, but she tensed up whenever I brought up the topic. I knew that when the time was right, she would let me in and until then I'd be here waiting.

I watched her enter my office, the sway of her hips enticing me and taking my mind to places it shouldn't go at the office. Steve had warned us on more than one occasion to ensure that we kept things professional at the office. She made that hard to do in that fitting gray suit dress and killer black heels. I imagined taking her right there on my table. Exploring her like I did the manuscripts before me. I wondered why she ever kept this side of her hidden. Still, there were other times when I missed the girl-like woman in the hoodie and Chuck Taylors that drank strawberry tea and laughed shyly.

"You ready for lunch Jake?" she asked, smiling at me seductively.

"I am, babe," I logged off my computer and grabbed my coat.

She slipped her hand into mine as we made our way out to the front of the office building. I expected her to walk to our café, but she didn't. Instead, she walked into another restaurant. We hadn't been to this one before. She motioned for a waiter and asked for a table at the back. I felt slightly bothered at the feeling I got of tailing along. But with one wink and smile from her I'd forgotten all about it. I sat across from her and took her hand in mine.

"I'm glad you're okay," I looked into her ebony gaze. Her eyes are beautiful, but lately, they look like they're on fire. How was it possible for an already gorgeous woman to look even more breathtaking?

"Thank you, Jake," she smiled. "So am I."

We ordered lunch, a plain green salad for her and still water and a chicken sandwich for me. I watched as she meticulously cut her lettuce and I missed her gulping down her sandwiches, laughing with a mouth full of food.

My phone rang, and I looked at it. I didn't want to answer it at lunch, but I was somewhat obliged to. It's Melissa.

"Hey, Melissa," I answered.

"Jake, you need to come to the hospital, its Mom; she's not doing too well."

"What's wrong with her?" I asked worriedly.

"Just hurry Jake, get here as fast as you can okay?" She whispered into the phone, and I could hear that she was holding back tears. She sounded so shaken and unlike Melissa Cole that I knew I need to leave.

"I'll be there soon Mel, just hang in there." I cut the call staring at my screen for a long time. There were so many emotions running through me all at once. I shouldn't be worried, my mother was okay, and she'd left a message for me just yesterday.

I looked at Sage, and I took a deep breath in.

"That was my sister. I've got to see my Mom, Sage, she isn't well. I can't expect you to up and leave since you just got here but I will keep you posted."

She took my hand in hers. "I really hope everything turns out okay Jake, I'm sorry." She held my hand tightly.

We stood, and I hugged her. I rushed out to the basement parking. I would text Steve on the way. I just hoped I was not too late. Please don't let me be too late.

"I don't want you to leave like this Jacob," my mother said calmly from the doorway. "He never meant any of those things. He loves you all so much. He just doesn't know how to show it."

I continued to throw my clothes into my suitcase. "I don't need you to take his side yet again mom. What I want is for you to leave me alone and let me pack my shit and leave. I have never been good enough for Dad, you or this family." I shouted at her and she shrunk back.

"I'm sorry if you feel that way, Jacob," she said sadly.

"I don't feel that way mother, that is how it is," I growled. "You never had time for me. You never celebrated any of my accomplishments. It's like I never existed. You got your pigeon pair when Mel arrived, and I was just an outsider, don't try to deny it. I could never measure up to your golden children could I?"

She turned away from me sadly, and I watched her shoulders heaved.

I am tired of feeling sorry for her, and I am tired of being part of a family that feels like it isn't even mine.

I needed to leave and go out on my own. They never gave me the recognition I deserved; nothing was ever good enough. Nothing measured up to their perfect children. You didn't hear them brag about my distinctions received or awards. You never heard about my published articles or my college degree. No, you only heard about the heart surgeon and the attorney. Not Jake. Jake fucking who?

I brushed past her without as much as a second glance.

"Jake, please," she pleaded. "I love you."

I kept walking, and I wiped at the tears falling down my face. This was fucking hard.

I never spoke to her since. It's been two whole years. I never called them on their birthdays or over the holidays. I didn't need family if that's what family was. I listened to her voicemails, read her messages and thought about her often. But I'd been hurt, and there was no way anyone could take that back. Still her last words to me were always I love you.

THIRTY-THREE

SAGE

I wished he were here. I wondered if I should be there with him. He didn't ask me to go, but then again, I didn't know his family at all. It would be strange for him to bring along a woman they've never met when this was obviously a stressful time for the family. I walked through my apartment, the familiarity surrounding me. I spent a lot of time here, but it never felt like my own. This was Siren's home, and I just lived here. I entered my old room, and my bed was unmade as usual. That frustrated me, and I started to tidy it up. What was wrong with me? That never bothered me before. I looked at the bookshelf behind me and started stroking the spines remembering the hours I spent in here. I thought about Siren and I wondered whether she was okay wherever she was. Jake often asked me about her and there wasn't a day she didn't cross my mind or what happened at the water tower. The things my grandmother said made no sense, the lengths Siren had gone to, to torment me. She was insane, and all this time I thought I was. I shifted the bookshelf and noticed my makeshift safe was as I left it, except one item was missing. I wondered whether it would surface someday when I least expected it. I pulled out my whiskey stash and the glass I kept with it, and I sat on the bed. I poured myself a glass and drank it neat. My throat burned and I welcomed the sensation. This has been my only companion for the last few years. I fell back against the cool covers and closed my eyes. I needed to stop letting *her* get to me. I was finally free. She couldn't get to me now.

I heard the laughing before I approached the door. I knew I must be hearing things because Dale didn't live with anyone, let alone a woman. I knocked at the door, and the laughter stopped. It took a few minutes, but he eventually opened the door grinning. His smile faltered when he saw me.

"Sage," he said nervously rubbing his hands through his hair. He was shirtless and absolutely gorgeous. His short hair stood up in spikes; his gray eyes were focused on me. "What are you doing here?" he asked.

"I'm here to see you silly," I laughed. He didn't laugh back. Instead, he stepped into the hallway and closed the door behind him slowly.

"Aren't you going to ask me in?" I asked confused. The look on his face told me all I needed to know.

"I have company Sage," he said plainly.

"You have company?" I asked. It was then that she opened the door in nothing but one of his white t-shirts. One of the t-shirts I'd drowned in. Her perfect tits were almost visible through the thin material.

She had blue-black hair and black eyes that sparkled. She looked vaguely familiar. She was taller than me by a few inches and so much more curvaceous. She was smiling, but her smile dropped the moment she saw me. She backed away pushing the door closed.

"Dale?" I asked barely able to get his name out.

"I'm sorry Sage, I wanted to tell you sooner – "he started. "-Not like this."

"You've been seeing her too?" I asked shocked. "How long Dale? How fucking long?"

"I didn't plan it Sage. It just kind of happened. We've been seeing each other for a few weeks now. I was going to tell you, I was," he said.

"When Dale? When were you going to tell me? Last night after you fucked me right?" I asked still stunned.

He ran his hands through his hair.

"You should leave, Sage," he said coldly. His eyes held none of the familiar playfulness and what I was dumb enough to think was love.

"Why, Dale? Why?" I asked him desperate to know how he could do something like that to me.

"Because you suffocate me, Sage, I can't breathe with you." He shouted. "You want all these things, and I thought I wanted them too, but we're young, and I can't do any of the things you want to do right now."

"The things we wanted to Dale, we," I corrected him. I felt like this was some sick joke like I would wake up any minute, and it'd all be on me.

"Leave Sage, before I say things that you don't want to hear," he said indifferently. "I don't love you anymore. I don't know if I ever truly did, I've met someone. Stacey is good for me. She's my muse."

I don't wait for him to finish. I turned around, to leave and then I saw it. I felt like I was not in control of my actions anymore.

Within seconds the fire extinguisher was in my hands. I turned around and started walking towards him, getting right behind him in seconds as he's about to open the door to the apartment.

"I'm not done, Dale," I hissed.

He turned around sharply. "What the – "he started, but I hit him on the head with the extinguisher. He howled, it was gut wrenching sound, the pain was obviously too much for him. He fell, and the door opened. Stacey looked at me with large eyes, filled with fear when she looked down at Dale on the floor close to unconscious.

"What have you done?" her voice was shaky. Her eyes stared at me in disbelief.

It was then that I felt it, pure rage, I looked at her and straddled him, lifting the extinguisher up over my head, and I hit him again without taking my eyes off her. The elation I felt was overwhelming.

His blood splashed all over the front of my shirt. It was everywhere. Stacey was still standing there like a mannequin, motionless. She was scared shitless, and I liked it.

She finally let out a gut hurling scream and rushed inside slamming the door. She's calling the cops no doubt.

"That isn't very nice," I laughed.

I hit him a few more times until I wasn't sure if he was passed out or dead. And rights then I realize I don't give a fuck. The bastard deserved every hit. I dropped the extinguisher and got up, and I ran. I needed to get home.

I woke up, and it's dark. I must have dozed off. I was covered in sweat from my head to my toes. I felt like I was suffocating and the gray walls were closing in on me. I struggled to suck in air, so I rolled to the side. The dream, it was just a dream, but I remembered it so vividly. It felt so real. Siren was responsible for all of that. She was the one who assaulted Dale. Everything that happened in that dream made no sense. Stacey wasn't even in the picture then but why do I feel so restless about it all. There was only one way to find out, it would be a long shot, but I had to. I got up and walked into Sirens room and started up her computer. It felt odd being in here. There was only one person that could help me make some sense of this, one person that I chose never to see again but this time, I had no choice. I needed to do this.

For me.

For Jake.

For our future.

THIRTY-FOUR

SAGE

The house isn't large. It's simple but beautiful. The lawn was well maintained, and the landscaping was immaculate. It wasn't anything I'd ever imagined him living in. But in all honesty, I hadn't given him much thought over the years. I don't have to be a genius to know that he's upper middle class, that and the fact that I'd done my homework. Siren's computer had a whole lot of information that shouldn't be there, it was just a matter of knowing where to look, and after years of watching her silently, I knew where to look. Siren had a habit of holding a bounty over everyone, I didn't quite understand the need for her information on this particular person, but at this point, I was not complaining. I just hoped that I wouldn't need to use it.

The cab driver looked at me through the rearview mirror wordlessly pleading with me to get the fuck out of the car. I glared right back at him, and he averted his gaze. I looked at the pathway leading to the front door, and I felt the urge to tell him to turn back. But I needed answers, and I knew that this was the only place I'd be able to get some. I paid the driver and stepped out of the cab, slamming the door behind me. It's hot, and I felt the beads of sweat forming at the nape of my neck. I stepped onto the pathway leading up to the house and welcomed the shade of the branches of an old oak tree. The cab driver sped off the second I was on the pathway. I considered my outfit, a simple black chiffon blouse which accentuated my assets, a gray pencil skirt and black heels, perfect. I flicked my hair back and let it cascaded down my back, instantly reminding myself of Siren. I pushed the unwelcome thoughts of her to the back of my mind as I made my way up the pathway to the impressive front porch, complete with an antique swing.

I stood at the door for a few seconds gathering my thoughts. I haven't seen him in years, and I wondered how this unwelcome reunion will unfold. When I spoke to him on the phone earlier, it was evident that he had his reservations about this meeting, but I assured him that it would be brief and that it was important. I rang the bell and heard the sound of children laughing and running around. I didn't expect him to be married, but I'm not surprised. Other people my age had married and settled down. I was just the odd one out. I stepped back onto the porch and took a deep breath. A woman around my age opened the door. She looked at me with a mixture of fascination and unmistaken fear. I recognized her immediately. *Stacey.*

"Sage?" she asked obviously flustered from running to get the door.

"Stacey." I ran my hands through my hair displaying more confidence than I actually felt. She stared at me, considering what to do next. I was not surprised that he ended up with this bitch.

I take her out of her misery, "May I come in?"

"Yes, yes, please do we've been expecting you." She said overenthusiastically, wiping her hands on her apron. Charming. I sashayed past her and felt her eyes burning a hole in my back.

Long gone was the sexy boyfriend thief; in her place remained an average mid-thirties woman who'd lost her glow. Luckily, glow was all I did.

The house was everything a family home should be, toys littered the hallway, the sound of children laughing in the background, a television blares somewhere, and I gathered it was a children's show. I waited for her to lead me into what I assumed must be the living room which was large and surprisingly airy. Pictures filled the wall. They were the perfect small town family, complete with the pigeon pair.

"Sage?" I was caught off guard for a few minutes at the man who stood up to greet me as we entered the living room.

"Dale?" I asked, cocking an eyebrow. The young musician I knew and once loved had been replaced by a more mature version. He was still extremely good looking and oozed with sex appeal. His gray eyes were still penetrable, and I couldn't stop the flutters that made their way into my stomach. He wore black slacks and a white button-down shirt, also something I never imagined him in. The years had been kind to him. I had the urge to hug him, but I didn't. I blame sentiments and unfinished business for my reaction.

"It is good to see you," he offered politely, motioning for me to take a seat on the sofa across from him. I nodded and took the seat offered to me and seductively cross my legs in front of me. I noticed the way his eyes appraised me, and I didn't miss the licking of his bottom lip. He resumed his seat in the high back armchair, and Stacey took the seat in the matching one next to him, protectively placing a hand on his. She need not concern herself. I wasn't here for her man. I'd been there and done that. The scars from that relationship had long since faded and no longer marked my soul.

"I- we," he corrected, "- were surprised to hear from you,"

"Thanks for seeing me at such short notice," my eyes met his, and he didn't obviate. I watched as Stacey shifted uncomfortably in her seat. I imagined she feared me but this time for different reasons.

"Honey, you wouldn't mind preparing our guest a drink?" he asked her affectionately causing bile to rise in my throat. Flashbacks from the scene I encountered just a few days ago returned. How did I suppress that for years?

She glared at me and I cocked an eyebrow. Seconds later she dropped her gaze into her lap.

"Sure, honey, I'll get right on it," she said tight-lipped. I watched her leave the room.

I can't understand my hatred of the woman or my need to dominate this situation.

"What is it that you really want, Sage," he sighed without missing a beat.

"The truth," I said plainly.

"And what do I have to do with that, Sage? We haven't talked to each other in years."

"I know that, but I need a few gaps filled." I noticed the way his eyes roamed down my body, from my breasts to my legs. "I bet you'd like to fill a few of my gaps wouldn't you, Dale?" I smirked uncrossing my legs and leaning forward in my seat. "I just want to know, everything you remember about that night."

He cleared his throat. "I don't want to remember that night Sage," he retorted, irritation written all over his face. I sighed. "It was a long time ago, and I barely remember what happened."

"I figured you would say something like that Dale," I purred. One must learn to speak the language of men like Dale Evans. "Which is why I may have something that just might persuade you," I smirked.

"Quit playing games Sage." He snapped.

"I've done my homework Dale, and you have been a very naughty boy, haven't you?" he looked at me cautiously, not wanting to give anything away.

"I hear you've been promoted in the last few years, how is your boss man?" I slid out an envelope tapping it against my chest.

He looked as if he had seen a ghost. "Sage, you attacked me when you found Stacey at my apartment. I had no choice but to do what I did. I dropped the charges initially but when you wouldn't leave us alone. I snapped."

"And you went and got them to lock me away, right? How'd you do it, Dale? How'd you manage to persuade them?"

"It didn't take much persuading. I had to do it, to protect you, from yourself." He pleaded.

"No, Dale, you did it to protect yourself, to protect that bitch you were fucking behind my back."

"Why are you really here Sage?" he asked, his hands slightly trembling. I could hear her approaching, and I smiled. I opened the envelope I'd been holding and dropped the contents to the floor.

"To settle an old score, Dale."

I heard the tray crash, and I knew that she was standing in the doorway and caught a glimpse of my parting presents. She walked over and stared down at the pictures her husband had been trying so hard to hide. She's numbed into silence, and I took that as my cue to leave.

He was by her side instantly. I left them and exited the front door. I'd gotten all I needed. Revenge was a fucking bitch, and Dale Evans was just dished his.

I should be feeling sick about myself, but I am not. I burned with rage instead. What the fuck was happening to me?

THIRTY-FIVE

JAKE

Sage arrived last night. One call and she was at my side. I held onto her small frame as we lay on a king-size bed in the room of my youth. She was sound asleep, and I listened to the rhythmic sound of her breathing. The last time I was here, my mother was with me, and now she was gone. I stood in this very room arguing with her, not bothering to listen to anything she had to say. And then when I got that call from my sister, I arrived too late as karma would have it. I didn't even get to say goodbye. I haven't spoken to my father since I arrived but it is not like he was trying too hard to talk to me either. There was nothing left between us, now that she was gone. I felt a lone tear slip down my cheek and gather on my pillow. *I miss you, mama.*

She always tried, but I didn't. My heart was filled with so much rage, which more often was misdirected, that I didn't stop to think about what could have been done differently and now it was too fucking late. I held onto Sage and thanked the universe that I still had her. I wrapped myself around her and let her warmth sink into my bones. She was everything that was good in my life, and I would protect her with everything I am. Tomorrow we would face the hardest day of my life, and we would face that together. I knew that when it came to Sage, I won't be making the same mistakes I had made with my mother. I would fight for her with everything I had until my heart stopped beating.

I woke up to the sound of silence and an empty bed. This house was large enough that you never heard anyone else. It was like each room was an apartment of its own. I heard the shower start and knew that she was in there. I wanted to join her, but my heart wouldn't be in it if I did. Not today. She turned off the faucet a few minutes later and made her way into the bedroom. Her hair was still wet and a towel was wrapped around her. I hopped out of bed and gave her a chaste kiss on the forehead. She wrapped her arms around me, grounding me, reminding me that all was not lost.

We dressed and joined the rest of the family at breakfast. Why was I not surprised that everything was just way it had always been? My father sat at the end of the table reading a newspaper sipping his coffee. My siblings were engrossed in conversation and barely acknowledged us when we entered. It was as if nothing had changed. But everything had changed. Did he not notice the empty chair beside him? Did they not miss the warm chatter and laughter missing from this dining room?

"So you're all going to pretend this is just another day are you?" I questioned them as I took a seat with Sage by my side. She doesn't let go of my hand but squeezed it reassuringly.

"Jake, that isn't what we are doing, we are just having breakfast," Melissa said.

"That is a fucking lie, Melissa and you know it," I growled.

"Language at the table, Jacob," Derrick reprimanded. I glared at him.

"Fuck you, Derrick!" I flipped him off.

"Children, we have a guest and no, Jake, we are not pretending that nothing has happened. We are just trying to have a civil breakfast before the hardest day of all our lives." My father chimed in without taking his eyes off his newspaper. Some things never change though, like his disinterest in his family.

I wanted to bite back and tell him how much I hated him. But I didn't. Sage was beside me reminding me of who I was.

I hated funerals, and my mother's funeral was no different. There was nothing intimate about it. It was like one of those state funerals you see on television. There were countless strangers there to pay their respects. I wondered if half of them even knew her second name. Friends, associates, colleagues of the family filled the pews in the church. The extended families were lost in the crowd, and I didn't bother for small talk, so I remained where I was in the front pew. So many people shook my hand, it hurt. I received hugs from strangers, and their words of condolences went over my head. I wasn't hearing any of them. The one person I needed to talk to today wasn't in this room.

The service was short and to the point. Again, I barely listened. I held onto Sage's hand, and I didn't shed a tear. This world didn't deserve my tears. My father gave a eulogy with focus on my mother's academic and career achievements. I remembered her telling me once, that her greatest achievement had always been the fact that she was a mother to my siblings and me. He wouldn't mention that because it displayed a depth of feelings and emotions, he did not care for or possess. My brother paid tribute to my mother. I refused to speak. The words I needed to say to her, died when she did. Later when we stood in the rain, watching her body sink to her last resting place in the private Cole family lot, I threw one single red rose into the ground before they started covering her casket with mud as red as a ruby. Family and close friends in the hundreds gathered at my parents' home after the funeral. I didn't have the energy for it, so I packed my suitcase and left with Sage.

Later that night I made love to the woman I'd fallen in love with, and as she moaned my name, I asked her to marry me, to stay with me for the rest of my fucking life. She gave me her answer as we reached our climax.

"Did you mean it," she asked me as we lay on the

living room floor in front of the fireplace.

"I did, life is too short, and I want to spend every second of mine with you. I want you to be mine, forever and always." I kissed her breasts, taking a nipple into my mouth and soliciting a moan that was like music to my ears.

"I love you, Sage; there should be no doubt in your mind."

"I love you too."

There is the person you see in the mirror
The one the world can see
But then there is you
You must decide which version to trust

THIRTY-SIX
SAGE

It's not long now little one. But when I say it's time you've got to go. Do you understand that? The little girl nods. "I have to go. He'll be back anytime now. "I'm sorry, I never knew," she sobbed. I knew she wanted to say more, but she didn't, she walked away, and her footsteps retreated down the passage. The screams woke the little girl, and she got out of bed, she had to find shoes and change into her day clothing like the woman had told her to do, but she couldn't.

"Now, go, now." The woman's shrieks filled the house, and I knew what that meant. I opened the window as she told me to and I ran. I ran as fast as I possibly could and never stopped. Not when the rain pelted down on me and the wind blew tendrils of my hair in my face, not when the branches hurt my feet. Or when I stumbled onto the road and couldn't breathe. Not when I noticed the car headlights to my right, not even when frail hands picked me up and rocked me to sleep.

The nightmares didn't stop. Instead, they became worse. They were vague at first, like a cloud of mist over my mind, but slowly the clouds lifted and these visions were becoming stronger and more chilling. I woke up in cold sweats almost every night, screaming at the top of my lungs. And instead of disappearing, they remained. I remembered them when I woke, and I couldn't help but feel a connection to them, but that was what plagues me the most. The draw, it felt like I was being pulled out to sea. I just knew that I was reaching a breaking point and that once I was there; there would be no turning back.

Jake would hold me and rock me back to sleep. I couldn't talk about them because they didn't make sense, not even to me. Siren was off the radar, she was out of reach, and I needed her. I needed things to make sense again. Sometimes I would hear her in the recesses of my mind, telling me to grow a pair and deal with my life. That was exactly what I was trying to do. I was up late again. I'd poured myself a second glass of whiskey. I walked over to where Jake was lying on the couch, and I tossed a throw on him. I suddenly felt lightheaded; nausea came in waves, I needed to sit down but before I knew it, I was falling, I tried to reach out for something, to call out for Jake but everything faded to black.

THIRTY-SEVEN

SAGE

ONE YEAR LATER

"I wondered when you would show up," she smiled at me wickedly. I met her gaze in the full-length Victorian mirror where she stood admiring herself. She was truly a sight to behold in her cream naked back dress embellished with lace and embroidery. It embraced all her curves and contours perfectly. Her hair hung in a dark curtain over her breasts, her lips were painted as red as sin. I could admit that she was beautiful because I finally saw no difference between us. She was me, and I was her, we're just two sides of one messed up coin.

"You were expecting me?" I tested, taking a seat at the foot of the king size bed, folding my legs in front of me, my stomach turning at the thought of her with him when I wasn't and couldn't be.

"Why wouldn't I be expecting you, Sage?" she swirled around to face me, her dark eyes caused me to falter. I wouldn't let her cripple me, not today. "What I don't know is how you did it?"

I took a deep breath, allowing my erratic emotions to calm. This was what she wanted, for me to return to instability.

"You can't go through with this, Siren, he isn't yours to keep."

"I didn't say he was," she laughed at me, crossing the room gracefully to stand in front of me. "But do you really think that you'll win, Sage? That telling him about me, wait, let me correct that, about *us*, will change his mind? He's mine, Sage. Live with that." She exuded confidence. It flowed through her.

"He'll see through you, he'll see the beast that is Siren, and you'll be discarded like the trash that you are,"

"We're all hiding behind a veneer Sage, not even your perfection is exempt. Remember that. You fight me because you delude yourself into believing that you have a chance. You don't have a chance Sage, not without me." She turned back to the mirror.

It's taken me a year, and in that time, this bitch has been living my life. I don't know how she managed to shut me out but she did. She took over my life. This bitch has been sleeping with my man; she's been destroying everything, my life, my pride, my dignity.

"You do not exist, Sage, It's what I've been trying to show you. You think you created me, but it is me that belonged here. You need me. But yet, you tried to suppress me. You thought you'd won at the water tower, didn't you but you should have known I would find a way back here and when I did, I'd destroy you. You need me to fight your battles. You need me to win your wars. And that is why I will always win." She said looking at her image and grimacing. "You're weak, pathetic." She snarled.

"When our parents died, you couldn't deal with the trauma of it, alone. So you needed me to help you, you needed me to find a way for you to cope, to live, to survive." She continued.

"But you're not real Siren, I see you, I feel you, I know you, but you're not fucking real, and I won't let you take away my life," I said desperately.

"I am *you*, Sage," she corrected me.

"This is going to hurt me more than it will ever hurt you," I touched my pocket.

I pulled out the cold metal, and she stared at me in horror.

"You wouldn't fucking dare!" she shouted, her voice echoing through the room.

"We're leaving Siren, the both of us or I use this." I brought the gun up to my temples. I didn't think that I would be able to go through with this, but I knew that I must, if not for me, then for Jake. He had no idea what he'd gotten himself into, and it was entirely my fault. I was the one that let him into my life. I was the one who did this and today. I would be the one to end this. I looked her straight in the eye.

"Siren, you have until the count of three to leave, 1…2…"

She lurched for me, and the gun was flung out of my hand. I heard a rip in her gown, and I was momentarily elated. She was strong, but I have something to be stronger for. I staggered forward and grabbed her by the shoulders. She brought her arms in between mine breaking my hold and simultaneously knocking me off my feet. She straddled me, and I heard more rips and tears in her gown. She slapped me hard, and I saw a light in front of my eyes. *I must be strong. I must be brave.* I recited my mantra and reached for her hair, wrapping it around my hands, I pulled her towards me. I noticed the gun was a few inches from my reach. I stretched out my hand and finally had it in my grasp. She screamed, and it was a blood curdling sound. There was no way that she was going down without a fight. I knew that, but neither was I.

"This time, you don't get a choice Siren."

She struggled, the gun went off, and everything faded to black.

THIRTY-EIGHT

JAKE

"Where the fuck is she?" I shouted as I entered the waiting room she was supposed to be getting dressed in for our wedding. We were having a small chapel wedding. I didn't want to invite my family, and neither did she. This was supposed to be our day. There were a few people from the office who we'd invited to serve more as witnesses than anything else.

"She left, Cole," Steve said from behind me. Steve was the only semblance of a friend either of us had.

"What is that supposed to mean?" I asked him frowning.

"This is what she does Cole, but it is not my place to get involved. I just suggest you not waste your time on filing a missing person's report." He flung a manila envelope at me. I opened it in haste.

It's from her.

I walked over to the window trying to calm my racing heart.

I'm sorry Jake. I see no other way. Let me go. Always, S

I turned around and glared at Steve in shock. It was in her handwriting, but I didn't want to believe that she would do something this messed up. She had no reason to do this. I wanted to shake him to give me answers, but his set jaw told me that he didn't want to get involved in this. With this letter, law enforcement would laugh in my face. I scrunched the piece of paper and threw it in the dustbin. What was she thinking? How could she walk away from me with no fucking explanation?

I didn't want to call her, but she had a few highly powerful contacts.

"Melissa Cole," she answered formally.

"Melissa, it's Jake," I said. There was silence, and I wondered if she was still on the line.

"Jacob, is that really you?" She sounded surprised but pleased to hear from me.

"In the flesh, well on the phone, whatever," I sighed. I couldn't keep the edge from my voice. I was anxious. I needed her to help me.

"How are you Jake?" she asked and I got a sense that she really wanted to know.

"I need to talk to you, Mel, but face to face." I didn't think that this was the kind of conversation you had on the phone.

"Do you want to come over to my house tonight?" she asked.

"That would be great, thanks, Mel."

"See you later Jake." She said.

I cut the call. I walked back to my room. I've been holed up in here for a week, and it was about time I got a grip, got my shit together and got to the bottom of this. It's been a week since I'd seen her, held her, made love to her. One week and everything I had was gone, and I needed to know why. When I got back home that day, I walked into the emptiness of this apartment, and for the first time since I'd lived here, it didn't feel like home, just a space, void of anything significant. I'd asked Steve for some time, and he was kind enough to give it to me. I knew he knew more than he was letting on. I should be angry at him, but I am not.

She left with only her handbag which had all she would need to be just about anywhere now. She didn't pass by here because everything was untouched, just the way we'd left it. We didn't intend to come back here for another week. I had it all planned, a surprise honeymoon. I wanted to break something, but I think the mirrors in my home have had their fair share of my rage.

I fell back on my bed, not showered and unshaven for yet another day. I would have to do something about that though. I doubted my sister would appreciate a vagrant in her home. Where the fuck are you Sage? I closed my eyes, and if I breathed in deeply, I could still smell her around me.

I pulled up at my sister's Balinese style townhouse which was more like a small mansion. It was built to blend in with the tropical environment and oozed grace and elegance much like its owner. Curtains and outdoor furniture were scattered on the entrance deck, I imagined that when it rained, she closed up the area and it still allowed for a beautiful view of the surrounding gardens. She's already waiting outside for me and ran into my arms for a hug. I didn't expect that, not from Melissa. She beamed at me and led me inside her home which was even more impressive than the exterior. The beautiful contemporary furniture was perfectly placed. We entered a large living room, and I noticed a small table set up for two in the corner. The effort she'd made pleased me. It would feel a whole lot better if I was here for any reason other than this. Still, I sighed and smiled at my sister.

"It's so good to see you, Jake," she said sweetly.

"Same here sis, sorry it's been so long," I responded.

"I know," she said sadly. "I guess we don't have excuses do we, except that we keep away, in our own worlds."

"You look thin Mel, are you eating?" I laughed.

She swatted my arm lightly, and I took her hand. "It's really good to see you," I reiterated meaning it.

I understood the tears that welled up in her eyes. I guessed none of us had been the same since our mother died. I thought I was okay. I had Sage. I had everything I ever needed or wanted. It was strange how your life can change so suddenly.

After dinner I filled Mel in on everything that'd happened in my life, meeting Sage, losing Sage, finding her and subsequently losing her all over again. After getting over the initial shock of me not telling the family that I was getting married, she started taking notes.

She spent a few minutes on the phone with a contact, giving them all the details I gave her. I'd gotten the basics from her employee file although I wasn't so sure if the information was accurate, and I knew where her grandmother lived from the last time she went AWOL on me. The contact promised to have some information to us by the end of the week. That would be three nights of sleep until I hopefully had my answers. That seemed too far away. The longer Sage was missing, the more I worried. The worse the scenarios played out in my mind. The angrier I got.

"Thank you, Mel," I smiled, meaning it.

"There is no need for that, you're my brother, and I would do anything for family. She's really the one then Jake?"

"More, than I can express in words. Mel. I don't think that I can survive losing her, not knowing where she is or if she's ok. It's killing me. She didn't give me a chance." I answered my sister honestly. She smiled, and I knew that she understood. Feelings were not what the Cole's did, but when we did, we did it hardcore.

I kissed Melissa goodbye and made my way home where I couldn't sleep. Everything there reminded me of her. I didn't know if I would survive not having her near me again. As I expected, the police came up with nothing; she'd left a note. She wasn't the first bride-to-be that got cold feet. But I knew that there was more to it. So much more. I wanted to drive over to her grandmother, demanding answers I didn't even have the questions to, but I needed to wait until Mel's contact gave me a bit more background. The police couldn't find anything on her sister either. She and her sister were estranged, and she never wanted to talk about her. Every time I brought it up, she would close up, and I could tell that whatever happened between them was bad. Bad enough that she didn't want to have anything to do with her. I should have persisted; we were engaged for god's sake, I needed and should have known everything. I let myself be led by love and all reason went out of the fucking door. I should never have let her out of my sight, what happened between kissing me goodbye the night before our wedding and that morning she disappeared. I had all these questions and the one woman who could give me the answers was nowhere to be found. It was as if she'd vanished into thin air.

THIRTY-NINE

SAGE

The world faded around me. Everything in here remained unchanged. Every day was the same as the one before. The monotony caused me physical pain. There were times when I missed Siren. I even missed the jeering and taunting, and there were other times, most times, when I didn't. I was sitting in one of my sessions with my guard. I called him that, but he's just a psychiatrist. He was a special kind of doctor for special people like me.

The room we're sitting in is as colorless as the rest of this place. I's not as awful as the previous place I spent time in years ago, but all of these facilities are the same. They drain the life out of you; at least that was how it has been for me. The room was furnished with one padded armchair and a padded couch across it. I took the armchair once just for kicks but I was disappointed when it didn't seem to faze Dr. Luke, he simply took the seat across from me and pretended that all was well. In his world it was.

Dr. Luke was a tall man in his fifties who reminded me of Hannibal Lecter. He looked a lot older than he was; his hair was thinning and his waistline growing. I'd asked him his age the first time we met, and he politely obliged. I wondered if the weight of the stories he held for safekeeping had taken its toll on him. I wondered if that is what kept him up at night. I didn't envy him, not when he left here and went out there to live his life.

I imagined that he had a wife named Diane, something distinct like that, and a daughter named Lily, something pure and untainted. She was a few years younger than me, a newly qualified doctor like daddy or a lawyer, something fancy. He would have a dog named Spotty or some shit like that. He had a happy life when he left here. Did they talk about me over their three-course dinner as they passed around the mash potatoes? Yet another basket case he was selflessly helping. Did he tell his daughter about my love for reading, did he tell her that I wasn't much older than her?

Had he confessed to his wife about the one-time Siren resurfaced, early on in my treatment, when the medication wasn't strong enough? Did he tell her how she'd slipped her cotton gown over her head to show him her scars, the ones I'd given her? How she stripped off her underwear not caring that there was a camera in the room. How she touched herself hoping to get a reaction out of the one person I believed would defeat her. She'd hoped to win, the only way she knew how, she moaned and begged him to take her, but Dr. Luke had looked away, frowning.

"Put your clothes back on Sage," he sighed. Not an ounce of concern or irritation in his voice.

"It's Siren, Siren," her screams echoed off the walls. That was the day I decided to fight, not just for poor Dr.

Luke who was only doing his job but for me. Not everyone fell for Siren's charms, and that was reason enough to celebrate. There were some that were immune to it, and Dr. Luke was one of them. He had a special place in my life from that day.

There was a small coffee table between us with two glasses of water and a box of tissues. Why did they always have to have tissues? It was so cliché. I never cried. He just talked, and I listened. There was nothing else to do. Life was so lonely, so I craved the human interaction even if it was just from him. Dr. Luke had become more than a doctor to me. He was my friend. I imagined that in another lifetime, he could have been a friend, a colleague or a confidant.

"Sage, let's talk about high school, can you tell me a little bit about that?" He asked. It would seem like an innocent enough question except he said it like he already knew. They all think they know. They think that it's all written in those manila files they carry around. But it isn't. Not everything.

I looked out the window. There was nothing that I could tell him. I could feel her at the back of my mind, urging me to confess, begging me to tell them the secrets I tried so hard to bury.

I sat in the classroom physically present but mentally elsewhere. It was raining outside, and I knew that I would be drenched by the time I reached home that evening. The last lesson of the day was always the worst. Self-reflection they called this one, and I hated it. I only tolerated it because of Mr. Wood. Mr. Tall, dark and handsome, Wood. He had soft brown eyes and his hair that fell over his eyes. He was in his thirties; I could tell, but he was like Christmas in July to me. But he was a rigid bastard. He wasn't like the others before him, he wasn't weak, he wouldn't bend to my will, and that was what turned me on. There was no thrill without the chase. I'd spent countless nights fantasizing about Mr. Wood, touching myself to the sound and smell of him that I'd memorized. I knew that was just his last name, but I couldn't resist the thoughts of what that meant. I licked my lips thinking about earlier in the week. I'd waited for the class to clear out and stopped in front of his desk.

"You could fuck me you know?" I chewed on my bubblegum and leaned on his table exposing my cleavage.

"Sage, that is hardly the kind of thing you should be thinking about," he gazed at me over his small spectacles, and I had the urge to get right on that desk and, so I did. I climbed on and pulled him to me, kissing him on his full lips. He was startled, scared almost but I didn't miss the bulge in his pants. I hopped off the desk laughing. I pitied poor Mr. Wood.

I watched him now as he paced the classroom, reading something from a textbook. I didn't actually hear anything he said. Today was the day, Mr. Wood. I'd planned everything to the letter. The bell rang at exactly one thirty, and everyone started rushing out. I took my time packing up, and before long it was just him and me.

The clock ticked, tick-tock, tick-tock.

I pushed up, without my knapsack, I wasn't about to leave this classroom until I got what I wanted. I saw the ring on his finger. I knew what it meant and, yet I was out to conquer him because he was just like all of them.

He was just like him.

"I need some help, sir." I leaned against his desk while swirling

219

my ponytail.

"Oh – "he said simply, looking up from his papers and noticing a few of my buttons undone.

"It's our assignment you see. I've been struggling with it a bit,"

"What about it is hard Sage, it's your thoughts, there is no right or wrong in it."

"Oh but I bet it is hard, very hard Mr. Wood."

The clock ticked, tick-tock, tick-tock.

He looked at me. I knew that look. I immediately climbed onto his lap, my legs on either side of him. I felt him harden against me, and I knew I was so close, so close to winning. But I had to move quickly, time was running out.

"Sage, this isn't appropriate," he growled.

"And yet, you haven't pushed me away, have you?"

I bent and placed a kiss on his neck, biting him lightly.

"Touch me, sir," I said as innocently as I could muster. My nerves were on end. This was such an incredible high. I could feel his weakness. I could feel his inner battle. The turmoil this innocent bastard was going through made me wet.

"You want to don't you Mr. Wood," I purred.

His hands slowly made their way under my skirt. "You're not wearing – "he hissed. And within seconds he had a finger buried in me. I grind against him, needing my high. No, I must concentrate. I looked at the clock above him as he grinded himself against me. I abruptly got up and sat on his desk.

The clock ticked, tick-tock, tick-tock.

"I've been a naughty girl, haven't I?" I bat my eyelids. "I should be punished Mr. Wood,"

He stood up. "I can't do this Sage. It's wrong."

"It is sir, but I won't tell if you won't." I ride my skirt up *exposing myself.*

His eyes widen. The look in his eyes is feral and I spread my legs further. And just like I knew he would, he unzipped his pants, letting it fall to the ground where it pooled around him.

"Do it now, Mr. Wood, now! I'm safe," I told him.

He plunged into me, the papers on his desk flying everywhere.

"It's good isn't it?" I hissed as he took me right there on his desk. I could feel my high coming.

"So good, so fucking good!" he was out of breath, unguarded, just the way he should be. No-one should be allowed to keep up their defenses.

"No," I howled at the top of my lungs, and then I heard it.

"What?" he said out of breath, confusion written on his face.

"Mr. Wood, get away from her," came the voice of the Principal and I turned to see him and a few of the other staff staring at us in horror. The man in me froze because I saw her. The woman who gave him that ring he wore. She's just there in the crowd. The tears fell from my eyes, and just then I let myself go riding on a high I couldn't get enough of.

I'd maliciously and calculatedly destroyed someone's life. He was weak, yes, but he'd been enticed and there were few that could resist me back then. I had no real reason to do that to him, except I hated men, I didn't trust them and I wanted to cause them pain. I only understood the extent of the pain I'd caused to Mr. Wood's wife years later. I hadn't given much thought to her. I wanted to prove that no matter how upstanding a gentleman they came across as, men were all the same. I'd spiraled out of control and I had no thought for the repercussions.

I wanted control and I took it leaving behind casualties. Mr Wood lost his job, his wife abandoned him and he was charged with assault.

"Tell me what you're thinking Sage?" Dr. Luke brought me back to reality. I stared out of the window. He sighed. "I can only help you if you allow me to Sage," he looked at me with those doe eyes.

I didn't want his help.

I didn't need his help.

I stood up and paced the room, standing at his large window. I promised myself that the day I got rid of the monster inside of me, this is where I would come to. I touched my fingertips to the cold glass. I would crash this very window and jump to freedom.

I'd declared myself insane and a danger to myself and society. I did that, and now I was stuck here until they decided that I was well enough to leave. I could start talking. I could tell Dr. Luke about all the things that I'd seen the memories, the brutality of them but why should I? I wanted to keep the monster at bay. I needed to keep her where she couldn't get to the ones I cared about. Gran. Jake. I smiled at my reflection, but it dropped the instant I saw her, mocking me, taunting me even now.

I hate you, Siren.

I hate you so much.

FORTY

JAKE

The clock kept ticking above my door. I couldn't concentrate, but I needed to get through these manuscripts, one in particular. The Author called him or herself Nameless. I wanted to ignore it, but the title and synopsis got me. *Siren.*

Nothing in life is ever monochrome. I discovered that a long time ago, and with all such lessons, I learned it the hard way. Dark cannot exist without light. Night can't occur without day. Despair can't flourish without hope. I couldn't live without her; she can't survive without me. She was meant to be my protector. It was us against the world. Allies. Partners. Instead, she became my worst fear. I allowed that despair to grow and fester. I let it mar me, then, almost destroy me. I realized something had to give. This time, there is no turning back. When the siren calls to you, you unwillingly answer. Question is… Would I survive the fall?

There was something about it that called to me, and I couldn't put it down after reading the first few pages. It seemed confusing, horrendous, even unbelievable but wasn't that the world of writing? It didn't make sense sometimes, but it did. There was no return address, but still, I had to give it a chance. Nameless needed to be heard, and I was going to give this person a voice.

"This makes no fucking sense," I growled at the man sitting across from me. We're in my office, and I was failing to keep my voice at an acceptable level. Ace Jonas was large enough that he took up a whole seat and some. His hands are crossed in front of him. His ebony skin shimmered in the light of the office. He looked like fucking Alex Cross, and he freaked me out, but I wanted answers and the ones he had given me so far, were illogical. There was no fucking way I was going to believe this bullshit.

He raised an eyebrow and looked at me like I've lost my mind.

"Are you even legit?" I frowned at him over the papers in my hand.

"Your sister wouldn't contact me otherwise, so don't insult me, Cole!" He snapped. His voice boomed and I was afraid Steve would barge in here any minute. I needed time with this information. It was too damn much to take in. How do I even begin to take it in?

I raked my hands through my hair looking at the information in front of me.

The report from Ace Private Investigating Services was clear and yet it made no sense. It meant that everything I knew about Sage Fenton was a lie. The basics were there; she was thirty-two, born on 22 September 1985. Her parents, Lester and Mary-Ann Fenton died in a Motor Vehicle Accident in 1994, after which she went to live with her grandparents, which explained why they were her only listed relatives in her file. There was no mention of a sister in her file or in the information Ace presented to me but I knew for a fact that she'd mentioned having one. She was an above average student with and inclination towards art and literature and obtained a degree in Literature. She didn't have a criminal record, but there were a few offences, drunk and driving with no malicious harm. It did result in her license being revoked for a year. I shook my head. This really couldn't be true. The next line stopped me dead in my tracks.

"This is bullshit!" I shouted. My anger misdirected at the investigator who is only doing his job.

"She was arrested for assault and attempt to cause bodily harm!" I shook my head in disbelief. Sage was harmless, she wouldn't hurt a fly.

"The case was dropped by a Mr. Dale Evans, who was her ex-boyfriend. She was hospitalized at Glenleaves Psychiatric Facility for three years after the second incident." The investigator informed me. "It's all in there. The diagnosis-"

"I know what it says," I snarled.

"I know it's probably not what you wanted to see, but there is no question of the facts. I have people who know what they're doing. A piece of advice, if your friend is in any danger, I would suggest you get the cops involved."

"I have, but they aren't doing anything about it," I said frustrated. "She's an adult, and she took off, so it isn't a priority right now. I was not officially her family so I have no right to make any inquiries."

But I am more than that. I don't tell him this. I just let my heart sink into my stomach as I go through the information again.

"Thank you, Ace," I grunted at my frustration with the situation, rather than him.

He looked at me sympathetically, nodded and got up to leave.

"If you need anything else, I'm a call away." He said before closing the door behind him.

When he left, I slammed my fists against my desk. Did I even know Sage at all? Who was she? These things couldn't be about her. Sage never drove. She told me she didn't have the time or need to get a license. I found that odd but there were people like that. I just figured she had a phobia and she would get over it some time. She waited for a lift every single day. I never saw her driving. There wasn't a copy of a license in her file.

She always told me it was her dream to get a college degree. Yet, she had one. Why would she lie about all these things? She told me she had a sister, but her records don't reflect a sister, and then there was all this stuff about mental illness and her being institutionalized. That wasn't Sage. She never displayed any signs of it. She was always so bright. She was perfect. Where did this information come from? There had to be a mistake.

I should contact Sage's grandmother and soon. But for some reason, I felt like this wasn't something that should be done over the phone. I grabbed my jacket and headed out of the office. I stopped outside Steve's door.

"Steve, I'm heading out of town, and I don't know when I will be back." This felt like Déjà vu, just last year I went searching for Sage, getting her grandparents address from Steve.

"Cole, you know that she doesn't want to be found right?" he looked at me with pity.

"I know, but that doesn't mean that I will stop trying," I handed him the PI report, and for some reason, I doubted that he would be surprised by any of this information. Whatever he was hiding for Sage, he was doing it to save his own ass.

"There are some things that aren't my place, Cole. You need to understand that."

I walked away, with only one destination in mind.

On the drive to her hometown, I thought about the last year with Sage. There were noticeable differences about her, but I attributed it to the fact that she was finally taking charge of her life. There was nothing overly odd about her behavior. We were happy. She was there for me when my mother died; loving her gave me something else to live for, to hope for. When I struggled with the fact that my relationship with my mother was strained before she died, Sage was the one who helped me work through those things. When I blamed myself she reminded me that it was not my fault. But sometimes I think that I might have missed something along the way. Parked outside her grandmother's house, I felt like this may be the day I got all the answers I'd been searching for.

The lady that opened the door for me was old and completely gray. She was a good few feet shorter than me, and I towered over her. She wrapped her light gray cardigan around her and although it was a warm day she wore a green polar neck top with a skirt that touched her dusty boots. She wore an old apron on her clothing. She looked completely at home in her surroundings. She was frail and tired, and I wondered if coming here was the right thing to do. But I had no other lead. The woman before me was my only hope. I had to find Sage. She needed me. I knew it. I'd called Grace on my way here, and although she didn't sound keen to meet with me, she agreed when I told her I was a friend of her granddaughter and that she was missing. She reluctantly invited me in, moving aside so I could pass by her. She limped toward the living room and offered me tea, out of courtesy, no doubt, and I declined. The house was old in every sense, outdated furniture, and doilies covering almost every surface. It reminded me of one of the old movies I watched from time to time. She motioned for me to take a seat on a couch across from her. She looked at me warily.

"Ms. Willis, thank you for seeing me. I know that this visit is unexpected, but I really need to find Sage."

"So you and Sage are friends?" she questioned.

I wanted to say yes, not wanting to get into more detail than I should, but I felt like telling her the truth would get me so much further.

"We're engaged, Ms. Willis, we were going to get

married, but then she walked out on me on our wedding day, and she's been gone for several months." Speaking those words out loud, made it real, saying it made what she did so much more earth-shattering. I leaned forward, my elbows on my knees.

The old woman looked taken aback by my revelation.

"I love her, Ms. Willis and if there is anything that you can tell me, anything at all, I'd be thankful." I sighed, hoping the old woman understood how important this was to me.

"She never mentioned that she was seeing anyone, but then again we have not been on speaking terms for a very long time. The last time I saw her – well, let's just say we didn't part ways well." She looked down at her hands, and I couldn't help but feel sorry for her. I knew that Sage's grandfather had passed away a while ago, Ace told me that. I wondered what it must be like for an old woman to be by herself with her only surviving family estranged.

"Why was your relationship with Sage so strained Ms. Willis?" she considered me for a second, and I saw that she was in conflict with herself about whether or not she should tell me whatever it was that she had on her mind.

"Mr. Cole," she started.

"It's Jake, Ma'am, "I corrected her. She nods. "I don't know what I can tell you that will help."

"Anything, anything, right now will do." I hated how helpless I sounded.

"There are things I need to get off my chest, but I

need to start at the beginning. So they make sense. So you understand. Everything I have ever done was because I cared for Sage as I did for my daughter." She walked over to a cupboard and pulled out an album. She handed it to me and took a seat next to me.

"My granddaughter moved in with my husband and me, bless his soul, when she was ten-years-old." She paused and seemed to consider her words. "Her parents and Sage had gone on holiday and sadly – "she paused and wiped away a stray tear, "On their way back home, they were in a car accident. Sage was in the car, and she was the only survivor."

"Did you find any information on her sister?"

The old woman sighed and continued, "We were close to my daughter and her husband and tried to see them at least a few times a year. Sage was a special girl, smart; she read a lot, even at that young age. My daughter often mentioned that Sage had an incredible imagination and she had an imaginary friend who went around with her. It was harmless of course but whatever happened in that accident turned this imaginary friend into more of an obsession." She stopped and looked down at her hands which were now quivering.

"It was okay at first. We understood that she had been through unimaginable trauma. We gladly brought *Siren* home with us. Even when she insisted on having two beds in her room and us setting a plate for Siren at every meal, we accepted it. We knew that it was a coping mechanism and went along with it to keep her happy. And we thought she was. As you can imagine, raising a little child, at our age was not easy. My husband was already ill. He'd had a few hip operations. We were not equipped for it, but we did the best we could because that is what family does Jake." She paged through the album. I recognized little Sage by her dark hair and eyes. She was beautiful, as she was now. Grace smiled at a picture, tracing it with a wrinkled finger. She seemed to be lost in a thought, and I let her be.

"Sage was a pleasant child, most of the time but soon after she moved in with us, we started to realize that Siren was a kind of escape goat for her. She would do things, terrible things and she'd blame it on Siren. Anything that went wrong was Siren's fault. She started personifying Siren, calling her, her sister. It was painful to see my grandchild losing herself, but I didn't know what to do." She started to sob, and I cautiously place a hand on hers.

"It's okay, Grace, you don't have to do this now,"

"No, I do, it's been too long and look where it's gotten us?"

"Sage started to get into all sorts of trouble as she got older. It was minor squabbles at first. She would forget to do chores, things like that but then she started getting into fights with neighborhood kids. Maybe we should have paid more attention to it and sought some help for her, but I only realized how out of hand it was when she started stealing from us and destroying sentimental things at home. As with most families, these incidents started to cause a rift between us. The school started calling more. She was getting into trouble for everything from leaking test papers to other more serious things -." She stopped and asked if she could get us something to drink. I could see that this was taking a toll on her. I nodded.

I paged through the rest of the album slowly. I couldn't imagine Sage doing any of these things, my sweet Sage. If I was desperate to find her before, this was the adrenalin rush I needed.

Ms. Willis returned with a pitcher of lemonade for the both of us. Anyone outside looking in would think that we had a perfectly usual catch up. But it was so much more than that.

"Sage left to college just after one of the biggest fallouts we have ever had. I asked her never to return here; this was not her home anymore. She'd done things Jake which we didn't condone, things that hurt other people. I transferred her trust funds over to her, and that was it. I saw her again when she got into trouble at the end of her freshman year. She'd beaten up her boyfriend. We didn't ask for specifics. We just confirmed that she had mental problems and asked that they let her get the help she needed. Sadly, there was a second incident and Dale, her boyfriend at the time, contacted us threatening to press charges if we didn't get her admitted. And so we did, we had her committed because she was a danger to herself and others. I didn't see her again for years after that. But even then she still hung onto Siren.

We realized that there was nothing we could do for her. Sage was too far gone. I only saw her again when her grandfather died and when she visited here a few months ago. She didn't take the truth well. I always knew it would be difficult to stomach." She started to sob again. "I failed her Jake. I failed the only family I had left. Jake, I know you think I have the answers you seek, but I don't. I don't know where she is and if anything…" I could tell that deep down, Grace cared for Sage. She was just backward and didn't know how to help her. "My daughter trusted me with Sage, and it breaks my heart that I wasn't able to help her."

When I parted ways with Grace, I pitied her. I pitied her because she didn't take the time to recognize that her granddaughter was crying out for help. There was such a stigma attached to mental illness, so many misconceptions. I wondered where Sage was now. Was she feeling alone? I got into my car, and the urge to drive off a fucking cliff was real. I needed to find my girl and let her know that I was not giving up on her. I didn't care about the past. I didn't care about anything before this moment. I just wanted her with me. The signs were there but I was just too blindly in love to realize it. The way she never spoke about Siren, the fact that I'd never been to her home or that she never went out. Sage was trapped and I'd lived with her for a year without an inclination of the struggle she was facing every day. I remembered the manuscript, Siren, she was Nameless. I banged my hands against the steering wheel. I had to find her.

FORTY-ONE

SAGE

I thought about him more often than I cared to admit. Our time together seemed like a distant memory. I didn't want to leave him, but *she* left me no choice. A person like me didn't deserve the life that Jake was offering me. I had nothing to offer him but chaos, and he deserved better. I belonged here, alone. Away from anyone and anything she could destroy. She wanted to take away my heart and soul, and I wouldn't let her. I would rather die a slow death within these walls than leave him to her. How did I not recognize the hold she had on me? According to Dr. Luke, the only way to heal was to admit that there was some trauma and that my mind couldn't handle that pain. There was no me and Siren. We were one person. He tried to make me understand that we aren't separate entities, but one-unit with differing thoughts, views, and responses to the challenges in life. But it's not as simple as that. The things *she* or we have done were unthinkable.

This was how I had lived my whole life. This was the only reality I knew. Me and Siren. I was starting to understand that this was not the way things really were but what I didn't tell Dr. Luke is that I feel her lurking, just below the surface, menacing and threatening. The medication was the only thing that kept her at bay. It was difficult to differentiate sometimes. I mean I could not deny the facts but what I felt was a complete contrast. I created her and yet she was the one that ruled me for most of my life. She was the one that in many ways still did. There were all sorts of non-conclusive scientific terms for my condition, but I didn't seem to fit into any single mold. The truth was that there was a part of me that was Siren and I had to acknowledge that.

There was a part of me that was angry and vengeful at the way my life turned out.

A part of me that was dark and cold.

I hated her so much but realized that she protected me from a lot of hurt and pain. She took the impact, and I was shielded. But, was that a good thing?

I didn't notice the changes in me a year ago, I slipped away into nothing, and I let her take control of my life, of my relationship, of everything. It was like I'd been asleep, in my consciousness, detached from my own life for months and she was at the forefront, pretending to be me. She was me. I corrected myself, a darker more sadistic version, but still me. She was there for him when I couldn't be and I hated to admit it, but I knew she loved him. I could feel it. I didn't know that she was capable of love, but she was.

The memories of their year together plagued me, she wanted me to see them, and she wanted me to doubt his love for me. When she took over she continued to behave the way I did but with that Siren flair. As time went by though she started to extend more of herself and that was when she felt it, what I felt for him. She stopped seeing him as a threat, she understood that he loved me, us.

Often, I wondered how I lived with Siren all those years as a separate person and not know that it was all self-created. We just kind of took turns at being the different versions of me, and I wasn't aware that it was happening. That became my life; it was all I knew. It was like I existed in a different plane from everyone else. Dr. Luke and I have had to work through that every single day, and I still can't marry the concept. The things she's – I've done, as Siren were inconceivable. I battled with myself all those years. I suppressed myself. I hurt myself. But now, within these walls, I was safe, he was safe, from her.

He was safe from me.

"The mind is a mysterious thing Sage, there are some things that not even science or medicine can explain, but it doesn't mean it doesn't exist." Dr. Luke told me.

I've started speaking to Dr. Luke. He isn't the one that is the monster. No, the monsters lurked just beneath the surface of my mind. They drained me; they devoured me from the inside out. Each time I closed my eyes I saw them, the monsters from my past, the monsters from my present, the monsters that await me. The ones I kept under lock and key. But it was time to open the vault. It was time to set them free. I knew that now, but it meant facing my greatest fear. Her.

We're in Dr. Luke's office again. The medication was wearing off slowly. I barely slept last night. I tossed and turned. And it had nothing to do with the uncomfortable mattress. I could hear her in my head. I could feel her clawing her way out. In the end, I forced myself awake and lay staring at the ceiling. The nights were the worst, they always have been. I have not rested since I arrived here. It wasn't just the fact that nurses came in every hour to check on me, it wasn't because of a lack of comfort; it was the silence, the silence out there clashed with the raucous in my mind.

I sat across Dr. Luke and took deep breaths the way he'd told me to.

"Be calm Sage. You're in charge here remember," he reminded me.

I felt my chest tightening. My breathing became more erratic. I scratched at nonexistent sores on my hands and knees. She would come, and we would meet face to face after months. I knew what that would mean for me and yet I agreed to this new form of therapy. Where I faced my fear instead of cowering away from it. I closed my eyes. 3, 2, 1...

"You're a state, Sage," she laughed. I opened my eyes and I was still in Dr. Luke's office. She's sitting on the other end of the two-seat couch considering me. I shrunk closer to my armrest afraid to touch her. I looked away, afraid that if I looked at her, I'll disintegrate. She shook her head.

"Always the drama queen," she sneered.

"You are me. We are one." I recited my mantra in a shaky voice. I glanced at Dr. Luke who was still where he had always been.

"You can do this Sage," he encouraged.

"You realize that he sees me, Sage, he just won't admit it, he's afraid. They all are? Like you, they're all cowards and fools." she rolls her eyes, shaking her head.

"You're wrong Siren, all they see is me!" I shouted.

She got up and walked toward the window, tracing her hand on the glass in much the same way I often did. She's wearing a black dress that fit her like a second skin and black pumps with a dragon wrapped around the heel. Her hair was loose and fell around her shoulders. Unlike me, she wasn't underweight or scared; she's confident and beautiful and everything I would never be. All those niggling old thoughts and fears came back to me. I felt myself shrinking deeper into myself. I felt myself falling. I wanted to run and hide. I wanted to be away from this place, from her, from everyone who thinks they know me better than I know myself.

"Look at me Sage," Dr. Luke's voice was calm as it always was. "Don't lose focus, we're here for a reason, you need to remember that." It was as if he sensed my battles despite the fact that he could not even begin to understand it.

She laughed. It's loud and filled me with that familiar fear. "Do you think they can help you, Sage, what is it that they can do for you exactly?"

"They help me fight you!" I shouted, with more courage than I felt, looking to Dr. Luke for support. He nodded, urging me on. "You don't have the control you once had over me Siren, and I have brought you here for one reason and one reason alone."

"And what is that Sage?" she sneered. "To tell me

that it's time we integrate."

She laughed again, this time turning around to face me. "Sage, you're always the victim, aren't you?"

"I *have* been a victim, a victim of you Siren!" I yelled. I was shaking all over; I had to hold onto the armrest to steady myself. My head hurt, my body burned.

She leaned against the window sill; all amusement was gone from her expression. "Do you believe that you brought me here, conjured me up and dragged me out of the depths of hell, where do you think I am? Does he make you think that?"

I sighed and looked away. I don't know why I thought this was a good idea, knowing Siren the way I do. Knowing how much pleasure she would take from my weakness.

"They can't help you, Sage, she retorts matter-of-factly."

"And I suppose only you can?" I resisted the urge to roll my eyes at her.

"Yes, I can, but you gave up that privilege the moment you made me your enemy."

She stalked towards me, "And now, you'll learn Sage, you'll learn why it is better to keep your friends close and your enemies even closer."

I closed my eyes, and I am confused about whether it's voluntary or not. Maybe she was making me do it, whatever it was I can't open them. I screamed for Dr. Luke, anyone but no-one seems to hear me. It felt like I am falling into an abyss. "Help!" My silent cries echo.

"Sage!" I hear Dr Luke's desperation but I can't see

him. He's panicked and I don't know what to do. "Don't".
"What have I done?"

FORTY-TWO

JAKE

I'd found her. It's been months, and I finally found her. I rested on my uncomfortable pull out bed in this dingy motel room. I couldn't believe that I'd found her. The flight here was short, but I felt exhausted like I could sleep for days. This was the closest accommodation to the hospital, and that was where I needed to be. I didn't care about the sound of the pipes at night or the greasy breakfast and stale bread. None of that mattered. Getting to her did.

I've been here a week trying to come up with a plan of action and build up the courage to face the woman that stole my heart and crushed my soul in the process. There was a time where I wanted to throw in the towel, I wanted to give up and let things be, but I couldn't. I love Sage, and that hadn't changed in all these months. I don't know what I will say to her when I see her but for now none of that matters. All that matters is that I found her. And in another two days, I would make her mine again. I visited the facility that she was staying in. She'd gone there after bailing on me on our wedding day. My phone rang on the nightstand, and I picked it up. Mel.

"Hi Mel," I answered.

"Hey, Jake, how are you? I couldn't get hold of you all day, are you okay? How are holding up?" I could hear the concern laced in her voice. "I could come up there, just say the word."

Mel and I had gotten closer since my mother died. She's helped and supported me in my search for Sage. I realized the importance of family, especially those who were there when nobody else was.

"I'm okay Mel. I just need to get some rest. Sorry I didn't call you. There are just so many things running through my mind right now, so many different thoughts and feelings."

"I know. Just hang in there and if there is anything you need, and I am not just saying that, let me know."

"Thanks, Mel," I ended the call and fell back on my bed. I needed to get some sleep.

So this was where she'd been, all these months. I thought it was a long shot getting Ace to check on admissions to psychiatric hospitals, but he didn't come up empty-handed. The place was practically off the radar, but he managed to find it. I walked into the sterile building, and I could place Sage here. Everything was so lifeless. Her doctor agreed to see me but I doubted that he would divulge anything that would help me understand what was going on with her. Still, I had to try.

"I am here to see Dr. Luke, I am Jacob Cole," I smiled at the receptionist who doesn't smile back.

"Mr. Cole I'm afraid Dr. Luke isn't available to see you," she stated expressionless.

"I have an appointment. I spoke to him a few days ago," I frowned.

"Will you hold on sir," she got up and walked to a back office to make a call. I saw her through the glass speaking into the phone in what I imagined to be a hushed tone; casting glances my way every few seconds. She returned and didn't say a word to me.

"Mr. Cole," I turned around and a brunette a few years older than me had her hands outstretched in my direction. "I'm Dr. Harris." She smiled at me. I take her hand, shaking it gently.

"Hi, Dr. Harris, I had an appointment to see Dr. Luke, is he around today?"

She looks around us suspiciously. "Can we go to my office?" she whispered.

"Sure," I cocked an eyebrow in confusion. She proceeded to lead me away from reception to what looked like a newly built office wing. We enter her office which is light and airy. She takes a seat at her desk and motions for me to join her.

"Mr. Cole, I don't know why you're here to see Dr. Luke but without divulging too much of information, there was an incident yesterday, and Dr. Luke has since been hospitalized."

"Do you have any idea when he will be back?"

"I'm not sure, there was an accident, and he sustained some major injuries," she looked down at her desk. "Is there anything that I can help you with? I wouldn't want to keep you waiting." She looked at me appraisingly, and I knew that she's fallen for the old Cole charm, despite the fact that, that was the last thing on my mind. Still, it could be used to my advantage.

"It's about a patient here," I started.

She raised her hands in front of her. "Before you go on, just know that we are not able to divulge any patient information."

I sighed. "I've just been looking for this person for a long time and this place, Dr. Luke, was my only hope."

"How do you know that this person is a patient of his?" she narrowed her eyes at me. I don't tell her that I had a PI who knew the right people to ask and the right places to check.

"I just do, anyway Dr. Harris, thank you for your time," I said standing up to leave.

"Wait, this is probably going to get me into a lot of trouble but who is this patient?"

"A friend," I lied.

She started up her laptop, and I sat back down. "What is her surname?"

"Fenton," I said more enthusiastically than I intended.

She stopped. "Sage Fenton?"

"Yes."

Her face dropped and I had a feeling that I was not going to get more information from her. "I'm sorry Mr. Cole, but I don't think I can be of any help."

I nodded. I expected that. I stood up. "Thank you again."

"No – I – Mr. Cole, please sit down." I looked at her, and I know that she's caving.

I take the chair for the third time in a few minutes.

"Who is the patient to you? Really? No bullshit of her being just a *friend* this time." She looked at me almost sympathetically.

"She's my fiancée," I sighed. "She up and left me a few months ago and a PI company traced her here. I called Dr. Luke, and he was willing to see me after I was straight with him about my reason.

She fiddled with her fingers, and I knew that whatever she was going to tell me would not be something that I liked.

"Ms. Fenton was also involved in the incident with Dr. Luke," she started.

"Is she okay?"

"We don't know," she answered me honestly.

"What does that even mean, she's a patient here, and you should know how she is," I growled slamming my fist on her desk which caused her to jolt.

"Mr. Cole, Sage stabbed Dr. Luke with a letter opener and pushed him out of his first-floor office window. She managed to climb down the fire escape and ran into the woods. Security is fairly tight, but she managed to slip through. They've been scouring the area since the incident and came up with nothing. We're assuming that she climbed over the fence and it's an open road from there, she could have gotten a ride to anywhere." She looked at me concerned.

My face must have reflected my shock.

"Isn't this facility supposed to be more than *fairly secure*? She could be anywhere."

I got up abruptly, and without another word, I left. I just spoke to Dr. Luke yesterday morning. Why would she even do something like that? I made my way out of the building and into my car. I drove back to the motel, and I ordered a bottle of scotch. I have never been a drinker, but this shit right here calls for one, maybe two. I sunk down on my mattress and picked up the phone. She answered on the first ring.

"She's gone," I sobbed.

"I'll be there in a few hours." I cut the call and took my first sip. This was fucking bullshit. This cannot be happening. Not again. I was so fucking close. I got up and slammed my hand into the wall. I don't care that I would have to pay for that later. I needed to let this out somehow.

If you do not disappear
They will find you
They will pick your skin off your bones
They will strip you bare for the world to see
Run and when you do
Never look back
Not even to say goodbye

FORTY-THREE

SAGE

She ran as fast as her tiny feet could carry her, she ran through the trees and slipped under the branches. The rain came down hard, and it soaked through her hair. She stumbled on some large boulders, and her hands were bruised. She needed to find them. She needed to get away from the woman. She was not a friend. She was unkind, and she'd brought the monster, she let them in, she let them steal the light. The faster she ran, the less cold she felt, and it was very cold. She didn't have shoes on, and her nightdress was thin, so thin you could see the skin beneath it. But she never looked back, not once, not even to say goodbye.

I opened my eyes slowly and when I tried to sit up, I noticed I was tied to a small wrought iron bed. The small room was dim and dusty, it was disgusting. I could smell the odor of dust, damp carpets and urine. It burned my nose, and I coughed, gasping for some fresh air. The dream, I hadn't had the dreams in months, and now they were back, again, even more, taunting than before. They left me drained and afraid, and I hated that feeling.

"Siren!" I shouted. The door opened slowly, and she entered.

"Up already sister," she laughed. "I thought you'd

appreciate the sleep in."

"What have you done to me? Where am I?"

"Always with the questions aren't you, always with the questions." She pulled up a wooden chair straddling it.

I struggled against my restraints.

"Siren, you're not in charge here. I am. You're not real." My voice trailed off.

"With all due respect, I am in charge because I'm not the one tied to a bed now am I?"

"Why, why are you doing this? What is it that you want from me?"

"There is nothing that you have that I want Sage. But, I can't say the same for you." She sneered.

"Enough with the mind games and cryptic talk, can you just say what you want to say for once in your miserable existence?" I wanted to cry, scream and bite back. I was so tired of being at her mercy. I was exhausted from fighting against her. I didn't deserve this. For once in my life, I actually believed that. "I went away to reclaim my life, Siren, to get rid of you, no matter what that took,"

"How did that work out for you Sage?"

"Not as well as I expected," I sighed and turned my head. The wall next to the bed was dirtier than anything I have ever seen. It was laced with grime and filth.

"Let me go, Siren, let me be," I said defeated. "You are never going to win, never."

She got up and moved over to the window, drawing back the curtains. Dust clouds were above us in seconds, and I coughed as it settled on me. The light hit me and filled the room. It's a dull day outside, but it's still more than I could have expected a few minutes ago.

"Do you recognize this place?" she motioned around me.

"No, I don't."

She looks outside.

"This, Sage, is where it all began, and I have finally brought you here."

I looked around me, and there was nothing familiar about this place. It was old and run down and off the beaten track. I could tell by the wooden walls and old panes. The pine trees that hang in front of the window make me think we are in a mountainous area.

"There are monsters,
living all around us,
lurking just beneath us,
soaring high above us,
Monsters, monsters everywhere,
Come and find me before they do,
Take me home."

She says those words and they sound familiar like I've heard them before.

"I know those words; it's a song, isn't it?"

She walked over to me and untied me. I got up and rubbed my wrists.

"How much of the truth can you handle Sage?" She looked at me with pity.

"I can handle more than you think Siren."

"There are things Sage, which you don't know, things that you should know. I never thought that you were ready for it, but neither has everyone else in your life. Things are not what they seem. They wonder don't they, at the hospital, why you are the way you are? Yes, the trauma of losing your parents was real, but there was so much more to it Sage," she sighed and took her seat on the wooden chair across from me. I could tell that whatever she wanted to say was difficult because it wasn't like her to behave in any way other than hostile.

"You don't remember a lot about the accident, and that is mostly my fault. I suppressed it because I didn't think you could deal with it. Finding your – our parents like that, she corrects, was disturbing." She sighed. For a kid your age, seeing the carnage, the accident resulted in was too much to bear. When Lester and Mary-Ann didn't respond, you climbed out of the car somehow and started wandering away from the wreckage. You found a way to get back to the road. You continued to wander until eventually, someone picked you up, a woman, and she brought you here. This is where she lived and met her clients. She was a common crack whore who exposed you to her filth." She spat the words distastefully. I looked around the room; it didn't look familiar.

Surely I would remember that part of my life.

"The dreams, Sage, "she looked at me like I have sprouted a few horns.

I think back to those horrendous dreams, the ones that caused me agony for years, looking around the room again, I gasped. It was the same room.

"How long was I here?" fear gripped me, and I feel myself plummeting. "What happened to me, Siren?"

"About a year Sage, you were missing for a year."

I laughed mirthlessly. "A year, did nobody look for me?"

"They did, they filed a missing person report, and they left it to the police, after a while they just kind of gave up as these things usually go. What were those two old fuckers going to do anyway?"

"What happened?" I whispered.

"You escaped, or someone set you free, I was with you all the time. You weren't alone."

"You passed out on the roadside, and someone took you to the hospital, and as they say, the rest is history,"

"Why do I not remember?"

"You suppressed that time. It was too painful to think about, so I thought about it for you."

"Is that why you hate me so much?"

She laughed mirthlessly. "Sage, you created me to hate, to wreak havoc, to avenge you for all the pain and suffering you had to endure. I don't know how to feel anything else. I don't know how to be anything else.

"None of this makes any sense. "

"I am your defense mechanism Sage. I protect you from the things you cannot protect yourself from."

I don't know what to say to her.

"Rest Sage," we will talk about everything later. She left, closing the door behind her, leaving me with my thoughts.

FORTY-FOUR

JAKE

"I got here as soon as I could, what do you have for me?" I looked at Ace who was sitting in a chair which housed him perfectly. His office was nothing like I expected. I realized that I'd watched too many movies; it was far from dull and drab with papers flowing out of his ears. Instead, it was housed at the far end of in an inconspicuous office park and very nicely furnished.

"I'm glad you could make it Mr. Cole," he continued to address me as Mr. Cole instead of Jake, despite my insistence. "There was something about the first search we did on Ms. Fenton that didn't quite add up. She enrolled in school a year after the accident was logged. That whole year lag just didn't sit well with me. At first, I thought it was just a typo, but I confirmed all the info. I also confirmed that she was hospitalized for over a month before she started school around the time she moved in with her grandparents. There is no record of her being hospitalized at the time of the accident. The police report stated that only two already deceased bodies were found in the wreckage which means that Sage was not in the car when they combed the area." He seemed to be waiting for me to take all this in.

"I did some more digging, and I hope you're ready for what I've found." He reached into a file already on his desk and handed me an old piece of paper and a newspaper clipping. "This didn't come up the first time, but I have a guy who is good at pulling out skeletons.

My hands started to shake, and I needed to steady my nerves because I was looking at a missing person flyer and a newspaper clipping about Sage parents' accident with the heading *Search still on for missing nine-year-old.* I feel like I would have fallen if I wasn't seated as the ground slipped from beneath me.

"Thank you, Ace," I managed.

It's been a week since she disappeared from the facility. I returned home and sat in my apartment unsure of what to do, and now this information comes to light.

"I have to go," I said making my way to my office.

I don't bother knocking but enter Steve's office. He's sitting at his desk, his reading glasses on, scanning a manuscript.

"I'm busy Cole," he grunted.

"This can't wait," I announced taking a seat, he never offered. "How much do you know Steve?"

"Not much Cole, I know about as much as you know," he doesn't look up from the task at hand."

"Steve!" I said louder than I intended, "I know you care for her, in your strange way. Just let me know how I can help her."

He sighed, and I knew that I was getting through to him. He removed his glasses and considered me. "You know Cole when you and Sage got together I warned you both, and now you're bringing personal matters into the business environment, and I don't appreciate it, but yes, I do care about her, despite the fact that she is a complicated and ill woman. I didn't meet the Sage you did, no, I met Siren, I interviewed her, and I fucked her and gave her the job. On Monday Sage walks in and she cried blue murder when I tried to kiss her. A few hours later, Siren appeared, set me straight and told me to keep an eye on her. She has this multiple personality disorder, but it's so much more complicated than that. I don't know more than that Cole, but I do know that Sage needs help for something she never admits is a problem." He shook his head. "Sometimes I doubt she knows it's a problem."

"She tried to get help, even checked herself into a facility, but that didn't turn out well. I just don't know where to look." I handed him the copies Ace gave me, and he looked at me shocked.

"I had no idea."

"I know I've asked for a lot of time off, but I need to see her grandmother again, and hopefully she'll tell me the truth this time."

"Take all the time you need."

It's raining hard, and I was glad I had the sense enough to drive my car instead of my motorbike. I pulled up outside Grace's house, and the porch light was still on. I ran to the door, drawing my dry mac jacket close around my ears. I knocked on the door a few times, but she didn't answer. It was late evening so she must have been getting supper ready. I decided to go around the back of the house. I should have called ahead, but I didn't want her to rehearse her response to me.

"Grace!" I shouted, knocking at what was sure to be the kitchen door. I heard muffled sounds but thought it was the rain.

"Grace! Are you in there?" I yelled. There was still no response. I walked back to the front of the house, and a red beetle pulls up. A woman with recognizable red hair makes her way towards me holding a bag of groceries in her hand. The rain hadn't eased up, so her poufy hair is now flat against her scalp.

"Hi, stranger," she giggled. "Well, it's a fancy meeting you here."

"I could say the same thing," I answered dryly. "Listen, I'm looking for Grace, do you know where she might be?"

"Grace never leaves home, which is why I am here, delivering her weekly groceries. Would you mind?" she said handing the heavy bag over to me. "Thanks, such a gentleman," she batted her eyelids while she reached into her pocket to grab a set of keys.

"What are you just going to enter?" I whisper shouted.

"I sure am," she said cheerfully.

She rattled the keys into the lock a few times, and it

opened.

The house was quiet.

"Grace!" she shouted. "I'm here with your groceries. Are you in the kitchen? You have a visitor." She sang. "He's a handsome one too," She looked back at me with a wink.

I shook my head. There were two things I hated in a woman, vanity, and forwardness because those are completely different from confidence and being outspoken. Some women took it a bit too far, and I had had a fair share of that in my lifetime.

We walked toward the kitchen; Molly leading the way. Just as she entered the kitchen I heard a shot and Molly fell to the ground. I rushed over to check if she was okay only to come face to face with Sage, my Sage, but completely different.

"Leave her," she instructed, and I got up slowly and made my way closer to her.

FORTY-FIVE

SIREN

I watched them argue, and it annoyed me. Sage should just shoot the woman and lessen her misery, but she didn't, she wanted to go over everything with her. She tried to understand. I am not sure what it was that she needed to understand. Her life was a farce.

"How could you not tell me, Gran," she sobbed.

"You were so young, Sage. You didn't need to remember that time in your life. I was afraid you'd be scarred for life."

"I *was* scarred for life, and you could have helped me, you could have helped me understand what was happening to me."

The old woman looked at her and shook her head, and I saw Sage falling for it.

I haven't told her everything, and I was about to correct that.

It hasn't been easy taking over Sage. Lately, she's gone and gotten strong willed, but I was not about to let Grace fool her into thinking that what she did was okay because it wasn't. She deliberately kept the truth from her. Her biggest failure was underestimating me. They called me Sage's imaginary friend, they called me a figment of her imagination, alter ego, a different personality, but in truth, I am her savior. I am the one that made **HER** life bearable.

"Sit down, Sage," I commanded, and she did as she was told

I walked over to Grace, and she was sweating like a pig. I hated this woman so much. It was at times like this that I was glad that I did not have an emotional connection to people because I felt nothing when I slapped the woman across her face. She whimpered, and it sent a thrill down my spine. This was what I enjoyed, inflicting pain and she was about to get a whole lot of it. I picked up the gun and just then Molly Kramer appeared. The shocked expression on her face was about as amusing as Grace's fear.

I aimed the gun at Molly and moved it at the last minute. I hit a cupboard, and the stupid redhead fell to the ground like she'd been hit. I was about to laugh when he appeared. I didn't expect that. What was he doing here? I didn't know what it was that I was feeling. Was it annoyance or joy? Whatever it was, it was new. It wasn't like when I was pretending to be Sage, no this was different, and this was him and me in the same room. He looked at me like everything in his world finally came together, like I was that missing piece. I could sense how hard it was for him to stay away from me but I also knew that we would both get burnt.

I am Siren.

I destroy.

I take.

I don't love because I wouldn't know how. With that,
I looked away.

FORTY-SIX

JAKE

"Far enough," she pointed the gun at my feet.

Grace was tied up on one of the kitchen chairs; her head lulled forward unnaturally. She looked worse for wear and I wanted to run over and help her, but something in Sage's eyes stopped me. "Hello Jacob, did you miss me?" She looked like Sage, and she sounded like Sage, but there was a chilling edge to her voice which was never there before.

"I have missed you," I answered simply.

She's beautiful, so incredibly beautiful and it took everything for me not to go over to her and take her in my arms. This was not the place for that. I had two injured women in this kitchen and the woman standing before me was the reason for it.

"What is this Sage, this isn't you?"

"You mean this is not the "*me*" you're used to or think I should be?"

"Either way, this -" I gestured to her, "- isn't you."

"Can you let me check if Grace is okay? I asked, putting my hands up in surrender.

"She's okay. The old bitch is just shaken. Your friend there is okay too; she just got a fright when I shot the cupboard above her head."

"Why're you doing this?"

"Grace over here needs to learn a lesson, and it's been a long time coming."

I took a few steps towards her, and she cocked an eyebrow. "What do you think you're doing Jake," she rolled her eyes at me.

"Can we talk about all this, without the gun?" I said calmly, running my hands at the back of my head.

"You've grown a beard?" she offered.

I nodded.

"I like it actually," she smiled, and this conversation seemed about as normal as Santa Clause.

"Bring her over here and tie her to one of the chairs and then we can talk." She signaled over to Molly who had already started to stir.

Despite the fact that I did not agree with her actions, I did as I was told hoping that I may get through to her and save Molly and Grace, that and the fact that I can't believe that Sage would hurt them. I walked over to Molly and hauled her into my arms, placing her unconscious body upright into a chair. Sage threw me some rope, and I proceeded to tie Molly up. I made sure that it wasn't too tight and then stood with my hands in my pockets waiting for Sage's next instruction.

"Sit down Jake," she commanded. I could think of a lot of things she could do to me sitting down and none of them involved a gun. She strolled towards me, and she was inches within my reach. I wanted to reach out and touch her, hold her, beg her to stop this madness and let it be just her and me again. I wanted to feel her body against my body. I'd waited for this day for so long. Instead, I did as she told me.

"That's a good boy Jake," she purred. She walked around me and got a piece of rope. I could quickly get away. I could overpower her. I could do all those things, but that wasn't the way to get through to her, so I did nothing as she bound my hands behind my back. This was Sage, and she loved me as much as I loved her. She may be a badass right now, but she was still the woman I held at night not so long ago when she couldn't get back to sleep after a bad dream.

"What did they do to you, Sage?" I asked. "To make you behave this way."

"It's Siren, Jacob. My name is Siren." She murmured.

"It doesn't matter what you call yourself, you're you, you're the woman I fell in love with and was about to marry. So I need to know what took that woman away from me. I want to know what broke you and then I want to be the one to piece you back together."

She laughed, and it's a sinister kind of laugh. I should be afraid, I really should. I have just put myself at her mercy, and there was no guarantee that I would make it out alive.

"Siren?"

She looked at me in disbelief, and I knew I had her attention.

"Yes?" she almost whispered.

"Why are you hurting Grace?"

She considered me for a few minutes and then took

the last vacant seat at the kitchen table. For a moment I thought she wouldn't speak, but she did.

"She knew," she said quietly.

"What did she know?"

"About where I was, all those years ago,"

"That is impossible Siren. You can't seriously believe that?" A lone tear fell down her cheek.

"So you knew too?"

I took a deep breath in. "I had a private investigator try and find you, you left me no choice, you left without a word, and I couldn't just sit there doing nothing. He just told me about that, and it's why I'm here now, I wanted to ask Grace about it."

"Well, she knew all about it, so you came to the right place. She knew he was a sick and twisted fuck and yet she protected him, she protected him for a whole year while he had me locked away in his hellhole. She didn't notify the cops, she chose her psychotic son over her minor granddaughter."

"Her son? But I thought that your mother was an only child. How did you find out?"

"It's what I thought too, but she isn't. There was a monster they created too, and I just so happened to get caught in his web. I guess I was just unlucky. She sighed. "I'm resourceful Jake. I have my contacts. Years ago, I noticed a picture in the album; the man looked familiar, it was the same face that plagued my dreams for years. There he was staring back at me from the family album. I did some snooping through the family papers, and there it was. If you're wondering, no, Sage doesn't know about all this." She looked down at the table tracing random shapes with her fingers.

"I'd wandered off. No-one could find me, but he did. He called my grandparents and told them he had me and they did nothing. They did nothing because they wanted to protect their son. And now I need to stop making the world pay for his and her sins. I have to make sure that she gets what she deserves and then I am going after him."

"It doesn't have to be done this way, babe, not like this,"

"And I suppose you mean the law that allowed a psychopath to run rampant. He was a pimp Jake and the woman that found me took me to him. He recognized me for obvious reasons. I was the spitting image of my mother, his sister, and so he called my grandparents to let them know that he would be keeping me as collateral until my trust fund got paid out to them. They made a deal to transfer it to him for my return."

"Did he…" I can't even say it, but I have to know.

"No, he didn't sexually abuse me if that's what you're asking. His clients on the other hand probably would have if given half the chance." She shook her head, trying to push all thoughts of what she'd been though away. "The woman, his partner, she wouldn't let anyone get near me to hurt me. But that didn't mean I was immune to the beatings and exposure to the evil that took place in that hellhole. I don't and never will understand why they took me or why they kept me alive,"

"How did you escape? you were just a little girl,"

"The woman let me go," She murmured. I know

to do." She stood above

"It isn't. You can sti

"Me or Sage?" she

"All of you, every

you."

"How can you? Yo

"I do, I know every

FORTY-SEVEN

SIREN

I was not programmed to believe anything anyone says, people are deceivers, they lied to cover their asses, to make their bullshit okay and because telling the truth was the most challenging thing to do. But Jacob Cole makes me want to believe. But then again he has never had to live with the hurt and pain that I have. He has never had to endure these nightmares. They don't plague him at night to a point where he cannot sleep. I have lived through those horrors, so Sage didn't have to.

That is my lot in life; it is why I existed. I watched as they sexually tortured the woman that took me in. I took the beatings. The scars were no longer visible but they mauled my mind. I was cold and untrusting. I knew that he meant well, but I could not allow Grace to get away with what she had done. She pretended to be something she was not, and it was time that I exposed her for who she really was. I have held onto this truth for too long. I have kept it away from Sage because she could never handle it. It would be that one thing that broke her and I didn't know if I could save her from that.

He looked up at me pleading for me to see another way but I couldn't. This world is full of injustice and misery, and I wasn't about to let this bitch get away with what she'd done to me.

"Siren, please," he begged.

I wanted so much to be the person he saw in front of him, but I was not. I was not Sage. I was not the woman he fell in love with, and I would not let Grace or anyone else live without retribution. No!

I picked up the gun. It felt heavy in my slender hands, misplaced. I don't have a heart I reminded myself. I was simply a product of Sage's rage.

"You are not," he whispered.

I still for a second, unable to think or breathe.

"You are not those things Siren, you are so much more."

I heard the coughing and looked to where Grace was slowly waking up. This was where the fun starts.

"Sage," she croaked, and I wanted to go over there and knock the wind out of her.

"I'm sorry, I should have told you," she gasped.

"Well you didn't, you didn't tell me, and now it's too fucking late,"

"It doesn't have to be," Jake appealed.

"Stay out of this Jake; this is between her and me."

"He couldn't hurt you, I knew he wouldn't hurt you," the old woman continued.

"Is it because he has such a strong bond to the family?" I laughed.

"Please listen to me, please," I kind of like the begging. It suited her.

"Tell me, grandmother, why didn't he hurt me?"

"Don't make me do this Sage, please," she sobbed.

"You owe me that much," I hissed. "So why the fuck could he not hurt me?"

"Because you're his!" she sobs. "You're his child Sage," she coughed, spittle splashing all over the kitchen table.

"I AM NOT, that can't be true. My parents died in a car accident. I am your daughter's child, you know that."

I looked at Jake who was as white as a sheet. He was scared for her, I could tell. He looked at me and held my gaze. I wanted to draw strength from him but I just could not. I looked away and faced the woman who was about to turn my world upside down.

"You are not." She said pointedly. I don't wait a second. I go over and hit her with the butt of my gun. "You lying – "

"Siren! Please!" hearing my name from his lips is a reason to halt. He called me Siren, not Sage. Grace was crouching over now, spitting everywhere. She's awake but very weak.

"You lying bitch, "I continued, spitting at her.

"I'm not lying to you, please, just listen to me. I have no reason to lie, not anymore. I'm old and dying Sage; I have to tell you this."

I sink down into my chair, hoping that sitting will lessen the blow.

"Mary-Ann had a medical condition which affected her ovaries. It started when she was very young, and it just got worse as the years went on. When she married your father Lester, they tried to have a child for a few years until a doctor ran some tests and confirmed that she would not be able to have children. Sean was 17 at the time, and even then, he lived recklessly, forever getting himself into trouble. In his senior year, a young woman in town fell pregnant, we all knew that it was Sean's because they'd been seen together a few times. She never told her family, and because she spent so little time at home and because she carried small, nobody noticed. They were into drugs and all sorts of other things and we knew that neither of them could be parents. When you were born, and Mary-Ann fell in love with you instantly, she gladly took you as her own knowing that her brother could not and would not be able to provide the home a baby needs. We knew about it but swore never to tell you, especially after the direction Sean's life took."

"Where was he all these years, why did we not hear from him or see him?"

"Sean got mixed up with the wrong people, and he got involved in some things he would never be able to get out of, he didn't want to either, so to protect our family, we made a decision that we would have to disown him. He was a danger to us, a danger to you." She sobbed. "Mary-Ann and Lester loved you. You couldn't have asked for better parents. That night when we got to the scene, and we couldn't find you, we didn't know what to do; so many thoughts crossed our minds. We didn't know he had you, not until a month later. He promised that he wouldn't hurt you but Lena, she wouldn't let you go, she'd developed a kind of obsession with you, she didn't know you were hers of course, he didn't tell her at first but he loved her in his own sick way and wanted to keep her happy since she brought in all the money."

"She was a whore Grace!" I snarled.

"I know that, I know all of that. You'll never understand Sage, what he was like back then. He was manipulative and cruel. I'd heard all the things he'd done but he was still my son, and I loved him despite the monster he was. He was my son Sage." she burst into tears. "He swore that Lena would take care of you so I remained silent, praying that he would keep to his end of the deal. I had no choice."

"There is always a choice Grace; unfortunately, you chose the easy way out." I spat. "Do you have any idea what I went through in that place? Or the things I was exposed to? You have no idea what it is like for a child to grow up in such an environment? It fucked up my head; it turned me into one of those monsters I was so afraid of. Your silence nearly killed me." My body ached from exhaustion.

FORTY-EIGHT

JAKE

This was a lot to take in. I felt like I've been thrown into an awful Daytime soap opera. But above everything else, my heart hurt for Sage. It bled for everything she was feeling right now. If it was like walking on shards of glass for me, I couldn't even comprehend what it was like for her. She sat there, while the foundation of her existence crumbled with a myriad of emotions flashing across her beautiful face. I wished that I was untied so that I could hold her and tell her that we would get through this, that she would be okay, but I knew that she didn't want or need that now.

"I'm sorry Sage," Grace said again. I'm angry at her. Angry at what she's done to hurt the woman that I love. "If we thought there was another way, we would have done that, but there wasn't. Your father — Sean, he wasn't the kind of person who could be a parent. Everything was done low key, nobody knew about Lena's pregnancy, and so it was easy to tell them you were Mary-Ann's and you were. She started coughing harder. "I'm so sorry. What we did, we did for your good. You have to understand that."

"Sorry isn't enough Grace, sorry doesn't cut it," I

sensed the change in her demeanor. I saw the sadness in her eyes, and I knew that was Sage right there. "How could you do that to me? I trusted you. I loved you. I…" she wiped a lone tear from her eye. "I can't be here now, not with any of you." She glanced at me briefly before untying Molly who was still passed out. I heard the front door slamming, and I wanted to run to her. I got up and tripped over my chair. It jolted Molly awake.

"What is going on here?" she asked when she saw me on the floor tied up to a chair. "Grace, are you alright?"

"I'm fine Molly. Could you untie Jake and me please?"

She hurriedly untied Grace who rubbed against the rings the rope left on her wrists. She untied me next. I needed to get to Sage.

"Jake," Grace's small voice halted me.

"I love my granddaughter, irrespective of which of my children she came from. I did the best I could, and it may not have been the right thing, but it was all I knew. Mary never wanted her to know, and so I kept her wishes even after she died. She didn't want Sage to feel instability. All she ever did was love Sage more than any mother who has ever carried a child could. I loved my son too. I believed him when he promised not to hurt her. I believed him when he said that she was fine. I was a gullible old woman. I have never been able to forgive myself for the time stolen from Sage." I nodded and leave. I wasn't the person she should be saying that too.

It's still raining, but I didn't care. I got in my car and drove to the one place I knew she could be.

It's still the way I remembered it. I climbed through the broken fence and trudged through the wet grass to make the climb. Mid-way I felt like throwing up, my fear of heights went into overdrive, but I had to do this. When I reached the top, she's there, leaning against the water tower, her head tilted to the sky letting the rain fall down her face. I know she's been crying. I can see it in the heaving of her chest.

"Go away Jacob!" she shouted. "I don't need you to make it all better. I don't need anyone right now."

I know that when a person wants to be alone, you should give them that. I know that, but I also know that she needed me to wrap my arms around her. I approached her cautiously, sitting down next to her. I wrapped her in my arms and allowed her to melt into my embrace. I have waited almost eight months for this moment, and so I don't stop the tears from falling down my face.

"I'm broken Jake, most likely beyond repair, I don't know where to go from here?"

"Why does there always have to be a destination in mind?"

"Because that is the way life is!"

"There isn't just one mold you know, just one way of living, one way of being, you of all people should know that. If this is all you have and are, then you've got to make it work, you can't keep fighting yourself, sometimes you just got to go with the flow. Let the fight, fight itself."

She snuggled closer to me. "But everything she's told

me. About my parents —"she sniffed, "Can I even still call them that?"

I drew her to me. "They are your parents, babe; they were the only parents you knew." She considered this for a moment.

"I just feel like my world has just spun off its axis and I had no idea how to bring it back to the way it was." She sighed.

"Then you give yourself time, it won't happen overnight, the things you found out today are huge, they change everything, but they don't have to destroy you, on the contrary, they are just what you need to get back up again. It is the moments that break us that finally help to restore us," I kissed her forehead.

"How'd you get so smart?" she smiled at me.

"Years and years of practice, Whiskey girl," I responded.

"Siren – I mean, *I* have done a lot of things that are really despicable. I am not the person you think I am."

"Sage, nobody is perfect, everybody makes mistakes."

"When I'm Siren, I do things to hurt people. I've destroyed people, their homes, and their lives. I don't deserve mercy or kindness,"

I gathered her close. "Everybody deserves kindness and mercy Sage; you just got to believe that you do."

"I don't, and I don't think I ever will,"

"Then we take it one day at a time."

"Jake, I don't know when she will take over again, what if she hurts you?"

"When that part of you surfaces, we will deal with

that, but until then all we can do is take each day as it comes. We can't base our lives on what ifs."

"She loves you, Jake," she wrapped her arms around her knees. The rain has since stopped, and there is a sliver of light above the clouds on the horizon. I can't help but feel that this is some sign, a sign of hope. "I didn't think she was capable of love, but she is, she loves you."

"Sage, I don't see you as different people, you're the same person, she's just a little highly strung, and I need to be on a constant PMS alert around her but that is the thing about your mind Sage, about the human mind, there are different facets of you, there are different facets of me. Some people can go fluidly through life, able to deal with the curveballs thrown at them and others need a little more than help, treatment or even medication. It doesn't make you weak. It makes you fucking brave. You had to learn to deal with the things that upset the balance in your mind, and you know that will take time and hard work. This is why I am here."

"I love you, Jake," she managed through the tears.

"I love you too SS," she beamed, and I knew I'd said the right things. I'd given her what the world and she couldn't; recognition, acceptance, and love for the whole and every part of her. The parts that will never make any sense and the parts that do. I knew we have a long road ahead of us, but if we took it one step at a time, there is nothing that we couldn't conquer, together.

FORTY-NINE

JAKE

THREE YEARS LATER

"SS, where are you?" I walked into the silence of our home. We gave up our apartments two years ago when we got married. The three-bedroom house in the cul de sac of an upmarket suburb seemed like a perfect idea, having decided that it was time to start a family. We're still a family I keep reminding my wife, but I know that there is nothing that would make her happier than to have a mini-me or her running around here. I see her sitting on the window seat, reading something, a smile on her beautiful face. I don't know how it's possible, but she gets more beautiful every single day.

"What is it?" I asked her excitedly trying to make a grab for it.

"A letter," she teased waving it in the air out my reach.

I laughed. "A letter from who exactly?"

"Oh, it's no-one important, just a publisher." Her eyes are beaming, and it makes me smile.

"Babe, just a publisher, that's huge!!"

"They want Siren." I knew what that meant to her.

After we left the company a few years ago, we started up our own editing and publishing business. The business has been doing amazingly well and has given us the time we needed to do what we love, and that was writing. But it was still a big dream of hers to be snatched up by one of the major publishing companies, and that dream has just materialized. I grabbed the letter from her and had a skim through. The crux is that they wanted her. They wanted my lady. Her story was beautiful, and I couldn't wait for the world to read it.

"We have to celebrate. You, me, champagne and a bubble bath," I said scooping her off the seat into my arms. I plant a kiss on her lips.

"I am good for all of the above except the champagne." She giggled.

"Wine then for the lovely lady?" I asked kissing her neck.

"Nope."

"Could I perhaps interest my Whiskey girl with some whiskey?" I kissed her lips.

"Wrong again."

I frowned down at her.

"Orange juice will do just fine." She suggested.

"Wait, wait, wait, and hold up, did you just say orange juice?"

"I sure did."

"Tell me that means what I think it means."

"It does," she said placing both her hands on my face."

"You're going to be a daddy, Jake Cole."

I smiled because the news was great.

I smiled because my world is great.

I smiled because SS was everything I could have ever wanted in my life.

I smiled because I truly belonged.

There was no doubt about it.

There are places between here and there
Then and now
It is in those places
I am most content
Neither here nor there
But present

EPILOGUE

I looked at my life right now, and I can't believe how far I've come. Just a few years ago I was a fraction of the woman I see in the mirror today. It was still a journey, and there were days that were better than others, but the fact that there are those good days was a victory. I've been working with Dr. Luke. He recovered and didn't press charges and surprisingly agreed to work with me again. I started a new regime of medication and we met at least once a week. I was not where I would like to be but so much further than I was a few years ago. Siren and I existed fairly harmoniously. I am Siren. I get that.

Four years ago, I married the love of my life, and it was our wedding anniversary today. We've moved jobs, moved houses and upstairs sleeping soundly was our greatest joy. My book is published. My life is full. Ivy was everything that was right and good in the world and I counted myself lucky every day. The nanny was on standby in the room next door to Ivy's so tonight was just for Jake and me. I still remembered the day we wed like it were yesterday, walking down the aisle in my designer gown toward a life and a man I had once only dreamed of. I still remember the feeling of holding Ivy in my arms.

There was nothing more I could have wished for that I didn't already have. My heart and soul were content.

SS, that was what he called me because that was who I was.

I am Sage.

I am Siren.

I am me.

I am the various facets that make me - me. I hated that part of myself for such a long time, but I couldn't deny that it existed just as I do.

The police found Sean. He was tucked away in a dingy motel somewhere off the main highway in a small town still running his operation. I found out that Lena had overdosed a few months after she let me go. Things had gotten bad for her, and she suffered the repercussions of her deception. I should mourn the woman who eventually saved me, but I don't. That was her repayment to me. I understood that. I didn't see Sean again, I simply testified on tape. Surprisingly, Grace testified too. I haven't seen or spoken to her in years. Molly wrote to us every few months, we don't reply, life was simple, and we didn't need to complicate it. I knew that Grace was very ill, but she'd held on now for years. I guess this was her penance.

I've let her go.

I turned off the lights and waited in the foyer. He would be home anytime now. I'd missed him so much, and all I wanted to do was show him just how special he still was to me. And he was. Jake Cole was everything and then some. He was gorgeous, sweet, kind, and gentle. He got me in a way that most people didn't. He understood me. He was my best friend, my lover and the best part of me. His sister and I have gotten closer lately. She comes around at least a few times a month. I actually have a friend, something I wasn't used to. I heard his car pull up and I glanced down at my new bra, purposefully peeking out of my low cut black lace dress. I've styled my hair to perfection. He walked in at exactly seven fifteen like he does every other day. He placed his bag down and made his way into the living room.

"Sage," he called.

"Siren," I laughed pouncing on him.

"SS," he replied, kissing me.

"Happy Anniversary, baby."

I've always believed in numbers,
in equations, in logic and reason.
But after a lifetime of such pursuits I ask: What truly is logic?
Who decides reason?
My quest has taken me to the physical, the metaphysical, the
delusional, and back.
I have made the most important discovery of my career - the most
important discovery of my life.
It is only in the mysterious equations of love that any logic or
reasons can be found.
I am only here tonight because of you
You are the only reason I am. You are all my reasons.
Thank you.

**John Nash's acceptance speech in front of the
Nobel prize audience during the ceremony
[A Beautiful Mind]**

COMING SOON

Fractured
David Blake

"Leave me alone Charlie," the young woman with the flaming red hair struggled, trying to get out of the big man's grip. He dwarfed her and was obviously stronger but she had spirit. I had to give her that. For a little thing she was giving him a run for his money. Charlie never had a way with these women. He hired them and didn't know how to maintain a safe distance from them. From the body on that one, I could understand why. Even scantily clad there was something about her. It set her apart from the rest of them. I could tell that her hair was not her natural colour, that she hated being here. I could tell that she couldn't be tamed and that made her all the more interesting. I took another sip of my bourbon and placed it on the table observing the exchange with amusement.

"You're a feisty one aren't you?" he snarled, displaying his sharp teeth. My brother was born an asshole; there was no doubt about it. He was the epitome of one in fact. He hadn't always been that way but growing up on the wrong side of the tracks, it was inevitable that he would be on the reverse end of morality.

She spat at him and I knew that meant trouble. He slapped her hard and she fell to the ground hard. Her small body lay crumpled on the floor. I shook my head. They were all the same, weren't they? All fight but when it came down to it, they didn't have it in them. I watched Charlie as he bent down to grab her by her arms and just then she struck her leg out, her foot landing right on his crotch. Man, I couldn't stifle the laugh. That was unexpected. Charlie bent over, obviously in agony. She got up and stormed out of the private section of the club and towards the stairs. I walked over and laughed.

"You dick!" he whimpered.

I laughed harder then, because in all fairness I wasn't the one standing holding my crotch right now. "Charlie, Charlie, that's a feisty one you got there, where'd you find her?" I cocked my head to the direction she went in. He coughed and sat down on the ground, pulling out a cigarette. "Tracey hooked her up, I couldn't say no to some sweet ass. She's a favorite amongst the regulars too. They seem to like her fire; I just haven't been able to put her out.

"It's because you're growing soft," I snickered. He glowered at me. I knew he hated that and I took pleasure in saying it. He flipped me off and rested his head against the wall. There were rooms lining the hallway but unlike downstairs the hallway had good lighting and I often sat in the seating area up here to watch the club downstairs.

"Maybe, you're not meant to put her flame out, I say flicking my lighter. Maybe you're meant to let her burn." He looked at me almost fearfully. "Leave my girls the fuck alone man," he warned. I laughed and made my way down into club leaving him to recover.

The club's red glow blinds me for a second but my eyes adjusted quickly and I sought her out in the crowd. She's a private room girl. I know that much. I was surprised that he hadn't had her out on the floor, first. That is what they usually do, train out there and then get promoted to the big dough. There must be something real special about her. But then again, my brother has been getting rather hooked on Tantalizing Tracey. She's an old flame of his who ran into trouble and he offered her this, a life of fame and a reasonable amount of fortune.

"Hey David," Tracey comes up behind me.

"I was just thinking about you actually," I answered.

"All good thoughts I hope," she purred.

"Only the best kind," I said. She was off limits, everyone knows that, but I could think of a few things I'd like to do to her. She's gotten arrogant since she's learnt how my brother *feels* about her. She's been pushing her weight around, acting like she runs this place. It wouldn't take much to slip my hands around her tiny neck and squeeze a little until her gray eyes start bulging out. She backed away and I wondered if she could read my thoughts, that would be thrilling, then she'd know what kind of thoughts I have of her.

I make my way over to the bar and the barman handed me a drink. He doesn't ask. He knows better. Everybody knows me. Why wouldn't they? My brother and I co-own this club but I am more of a silent partner, I earn my salary and keep out of the affairs of the club.

I have other things to handle anyway. I take a sip of my bourbon.

"Excuse me," the woman beside me tried to get the attention of the bartender. It's Firecracker from before. "Excuse me," she tried again and sighed. She tapped her fingers on the counter.

Up close she was even more beautiful. I have had my fair share of beauties in my day but this one kind of stood out. Her large eyes are magnetic. She hit me with a sidelong glance and looks ahead again.

I'm amused instantly. Did she just give me a *"what the fuck are you looking at"* stare down? I'd have to teach this little one some manners.

The barman returns. "Anything she wants is on me," I said tilting my head to get a view of her ass.

"Sorry, do I know you?" her eyes shot me daggers. "Cos I don't think I know you. And if that is the case, don't stare at my fucking ass and more importantly, I can pay for my own drinks."

I grinned at her. This was going to be an interesting one.

I stood up from my stool and towered above her. She didn't flinch but frowned. Out of the corner of my eye I saw the barman busying himself.

"You're a spirited one aren't you?"

"Excuse me?" she stared at me in disbelief and I picked her up and placed her on the barstool proceeding to spread her legs and take my place in there.

"What the-?" she's frazzled. I can tell. This always happens, they fight it but the urge to know more is there.

"I'm going to let you get to know me little bird," I hissed and when her breath hitched I brought my lips to hers and tasted her ravenously.

That's it Firecracker, burn.

ACKNOWLEDGMENTS

This journey was not easy. It was emotionally exhausting and tedious at the best of times. I felt like my back was against the wall, but I trudged on, and today as I type this thank you, I am grateful for every second of it. I would do it again and again and again, for the love of words and the love of the story. This story is very close to my heart, the topic of mental illness of any kind has been an incredibly taboo subject in society for the longest of time.

There was a point in my life where I failed to realize how absolutely daunting it was to live with such an illness. I refused to accept that it was as significant as any other chronic condition one may have but I reached enlightenment and I am a better person for it. We need to stand up and acknowledge it and accept that it is a very real challenge for so many people. It is a silent killer if not treated. Having suffered severe depression myself, I am still working through this every day. It is a constant battle, one so many must face and conquer.

There is no shame in it. There is no shame in seeking help professionally. There is no shame in admitting that the weight of it is sometimes hard to bear. The battle against yourself is the greatest battle you will ever face. To the Sages and Sirens of this world, I see you, I truly do.

As always, I thank my beautiful family, my husband Brian and my son Brady, thank you, for all the time you give me to write, for your love and support and just cheering me on. My biggest fans. Thank you for the laughter and joy and everything in between. I am so grateful for this life. You are forever the first people on my mind when I want to say thank you. I am grateful for every second with you both. I love you with my heart and soul and words.

Janine, Taryn, and Jhovehe, having you guys in my corner are everything a girl needs in life. My family and my friends all rolled into one. My people. My tribe. I can't wait for our book tour. I can see us doing that someday soon.

To my amazing cover designer and mentor, Dani Rene, thank you for bringing Siren to life with this cover. Your talent knows no bounds, with barely a snippet of a story you found her. Thank you. Thank you for the "pep" talks which sometimes leave me reeling but teach me a hell of a lot. You're amazing.

To my Beta readers and ARC readers, a special heartfelt thank you with all of my heart to each and every one of you. There are truly no words to express my gratitude for the time you spent on my book. All your comments and input have been so incredible and have taken this story to new heights. The feedback you have given me has been invaluable.

To my editor Jenny Dillion, I have enjoyed working

with you so much. Thank you for not just editing but actually reading and seeing my story. That is something I truly appreciate. Thank you for coming through even with the shorter timelines and a surprise novella popping up.

A special thank you to Janine Chetty and Brian Joseph for your incredible work proofreading this story, you have an eye for this kind of thing and I appreciate you doing so at such short notice and in such a short time.

To Jo's Romance Queens, my team, I am so grateful for all of you, for the participation, sharing, caring, laughing and everything else.

A special thank you to my babe, Nicole Townsend Brown, I don't know what I would do without you. You were my lead cheerleader during Infinity, and you still are. I have no words to express my gratitude to you.

To two special author friends, the talented and beautiful Auden Dar and Leigh Lennon, I am so glad to have met you on this journey. Thank you for the words of encouragement, for checking in on me even during your busy schedules, for agreeing to beta and arc read.

And to you my readers, I will forever be grateful that you decided to take a chance on me. This would not be possible without you. I would not be me without you. Keep in touch. I look forward to hearing from each and every one of you.

ABOUT THE AUTHOR

Jo-Anne is an indie contemporary romance author. She loves all things love and romance. She was a sucker for the seemingly impossible, second chances and everything in between. Her lifelong love affair with words started from a young age and blossomed to her debut release of Infinity. Her writing is and will always be her ultimate adventure and escape.

Jo-Anne is also an advocate for the infant and baby loss community. She regularly writes for on-line publication Still Standing Magazine and the website Glow in the Woods. Her articles have been republished in several newsletters. She has contributed to the book, Our Only Time, Edited by Amie Lands, Author.

*"There is no greater agony than
bearing an untold story inside you."*
- Maya Angelou

ALSO BY THE AUTHOR

Contemporary Romance
Infinity
Destiny (coming 2018)
Faded Hues (coming 2018)

Psychological Romance
Siren
Samsara (coming 2018)

Novella
Serendipity: A Christmas Novella

STALK LINKS

Keep up to date on
my new book releases and events:

www.joannejosephauthor.com
Email: info@joannejosephauthor.com
www.instagram.com/joanne.joseph84
www.twitter.com/jjosephauthor
www.facebook.com/joanne.joseph.54584
Pinterest: joannejosephauthor